CW01506569

THE BLACK ORPHAN

Also by S. Hussain Zaidi

Byculla to Bangkok

Headley and I

Mumbai Avengers

Eleventh Hour

The Endgame

Zero Day

THE BLACK ORPHAN

S. HUSSAIN ZAIDI

HarperCollins *Publishers* India

First published in India by HarperCollins *Publishers* 2024
4th Floor, Tower A, Building No. 10, DLF Cyber City,
DLF Phase II, Gurugram, Haryana – 122002
www.harpercollins.co.in

2 4 6 8 10 9 7 5 3 1

Copyright © S. Hussain Zaidi 2024

P-ISBN: 978-93-5489-997-3
E-ISBN: 978-93-5489-940-9

This is a work of fiction and all characters and incidents described in this book are the product of the author's imagination. Any resemblance to actual persons, living or dead, is entirely coincidental.

S. Hussain Zaidi asserts the moral right
to be identified as the author of this work.

All rights reserved. No part of this publication may be reproduced, stored in a retrieval system, or transmitted, in any form or by any means, electronic, mechanical, photocopying, recording or otherwise, without the prior permission of the publishers.

Typeset in 11.5/15.7 Adobe Devanagari at
Manipal Technologies Limited, Manipal

Printed and bound at
Thomson Press (India) Ltd

This book is produced from independently certified FSC® paper
to ensure responsible forest management.

For the two most powerful people in my life:
Reza Ali Mirza
Mohaddesa Zahra

AUTHOR'S NOTE

For this book, as with most of the ones I have brought before you, I owe a debt of gratitude to the biggest source of inspiration for my fiction – fact. There are multitudes of facts all around us that go unexplored or unacknowledged, but some of these do not sit well with people like me – cursed with wanting to tell every story that is out there, but often crippled because of the lack of a right medium. When I discovered the possibility of narrating facts through fiction, I resolved to let no story remain untold anymore.

For instance, it is a fact that the Indian intelligence community collaborated with the US authorities on several operations and had a significant contribution in the hunt for Osama Bin Laden. In the midst of all the cinematic and literary tributes – all of them justified –

to Seal Team Six and the Central Intelligence Agency (CIA), I felt that the role played by India needed more than a passing mention. The wiser reader might connect this sentiment with the angst the Indian spies in this book show towards the lordly CIA at the end. I can neither confirm nor deny whether these two are related.

But this instance, in truth, led to the birth of my protagonist Ajay Rajvardhan who, over the chapters, has also undergone several changes. He is my tribute to the unnamed Indian agents who were equally responsible in taking down Bin Laden.

Similarly, the mysterious deaths of eleven Indian nuclear scientists over a period of four years has not been talked about as much as I would have liked. The last available article about it – I did a quick Google News search before writing this – is from August 2023. The one before that? From October 2015.

This lack of conversation around something so crucial to our country bothers me to no end. These nuclear scientists were part of a team that makes our nation self-sufficient and indomitable. Their untimely deaths should be probed or discussed. If my 'conspiracy theories' cause even 1 per cent of Indians to go online, search about these deaths and talk about them on social media, I shall be happy.

The idea for this book had its genesis in some freewheeling conversations between Additional Director-General of Maharashtra Police Brijesh Singh, celebrated and awe-inspiring writer Vibha Singh and my humble self, many moons ago. Brijesh Singh, currently posted as principal secretary to the Maharashtra Chief Minister's Office, is a walking-talking encyclopaedia of knowledge about a long list of subjects, from cybersecurity, artificial intelligence, crime investigation and detection to espionage. I owe a debt of gratitude to Brijesh Singh and Vibha, because of whom this story developed into a book. However, I have taken a few creative liberties in the book that, if found inaccurate, should not be ascribed to my learned friends. I should be held solely responsible for any incorrect representation.

Retired Delhi Police Commissioner Neeraj Kumar is another name I must mention with an equal amount of gratitude. He not only injected life into the novel in the form of his wide experience and expertise, but also lent his name to one of the characters in my book. My publishers were not so sure if he would agree to this, but Neeraj Kumar was generous to immediately shoot a mail of consent. Neeraj Sahab, thank you.

There are also some I want to thank who will remain unnamed. A certain number (I could tell you how many, but then I'd have to kill you) of officers with the National Investigation Agency who shared a lot of inputs that brought in the authenticity that is the backbone of this book. As I said earlier, fact is the foundation of my fiction, and the constant battle that I fight is to not let one win over the other.

And, last but definitely not least are my own unlikely heroes, the people I met who have gone on to become valuable to my writing process. Kashif Mashaikh, friend and budding author, played a crucial role in the initial development of the story. Shahwaz Mirza and Ammar Zaidi took a lot of pain to shoot images for the cover. For the many, many small and large processes that go into the writing of a book, they are the ones I dial without a second thought. I don't have them on speed dial; they're almost always at the top of my Recent Calls list.

My young and patient editor, Amrita Mukerji, was a strong pillar of support throughout the book. It has been a real pleasure to work with her as she brings out the best in a writer.

Beyond the power of the written word is the magic of an eloquent image. Aashim Raj has indeed exhibited wizardry with the cover design of the book. After working on several iterations, Aashim finally cracked a perfect cover.

My young and talented protégé Mohsin Rizvi is a versatile mastermind par excellence. I can't think of any book or design without his innovative ideas and suggestions. Despite his gruelling schedule in London, he found time to keep sharing his valuable inputs for the book theme and design. Thanks, Mohsin!

Against the lengthiest and strongest of objections – and this man can be very eloquent when he wants to be – I am saving the best for the last, in the form of Gautam S. Mengle. The long-haired lost young man who wandered into my office at *The Asian Age* fifteen years ago has turned out to be the most dependable sounding board, protégé and friend – not necessarily in that order – apart from being a veritable writer in his own right (the long hair is gone and thank heavens for that). He has, over the last few months, been the bulwark that propelled me to finish the story on time. In the process, Gautam has become as possessive and protective of this story as I have, and it is this very love for fiction – which leads to him immediately adopting a story as his own – that makes him any writer's best friend. Thanks, Gautam!

PROLOGUE

The MH-60 Black Hawk helicopter, which had been steady in the air until now, began tailspinning uncontrollably towards the ground. Disturbed by the disastrous start to the operation, the agent took cover behind the compound's boundary wall. He watched as the chopper crashed. However, there were no casualties among any of the Americans inside the chopper because of its low altitude. Thankfully, the second chopper remained stable.

He was an undercover agent with India's National Investigation Agency (NIA). He had on a desert camouflage mask, which covered his face from nose to chin. A Kevlar helmet shielded his head. He had held many identities in foreign lands, but his codename tonight was Ghazi, the Arabic word for warrior. No one, be it the press or the common man, would ever know of this Indian agent's presence during the operation. In fact, the very involvement of India would only ever be known to a handful of people in the country and the US.

While the NIA had identified this safe house in Abbottabad, Pakistan, as where the world's most wanted terrorist was supposed to be hiding, it was Ghazi who had confirmed that their subject was indeed present on the premises.

Among Ghazi's many sources in Pakistan was a doctor who had obtained access to the Abbottabad safe house under the guise of vaccinating the children who lived there. Posing as his compounder, Ghazi had accompanied the doctor on several visits to the Waziristan haveli, as the locals called it, and stealthily collected DNA samples, which the CIA had used to conclude that Osama Bin Laden was indeed hiding there. The samples had been given to the CIA on one condition: the Indian agent would be a spectator to the raid. The Prime Minister's Office in India wanted to ascertain that their efforts to eliminate the fountainhead of terror had finally borne fruit. For the CIA, the deal was a no-brainer. The DNA sample reduced the possibility of mistaken identity to approximately one in 11.8 quadrillion.

Through his night-vision goggles, Ghazi saw SEAL Team Six fast-roping down the second chopper. He racked the semi-automatic assault rifle in his hands and made his way towards the rendezvous point. The commander of the SEAL team emerged in front and the squad formed a security perimeter around him. The SEALs had brought along Belgian Malinois military dogs who were trained for assault missions. From their growls, Ghazi figured that these dogs had already smelled blood. They were ready for the hunt.

'He's still in there?' the commander asked.

Ghazi nodded and held up his right hand in a thumbs-up sign.

'Stay behind us,' the commander said.

A controlled explosion of C-4 charges blew open the metal gate of the compound. A bearded man opened the house's door and the point man took him down swiftly. Women started screaming inside the building. The Shaikh, as Bin Laden was known, was fond of his women and had married at least five times.

Upon entering the house, a SEAL operator kicked aside a wooden cabinet to make their way forward. A magazine fell out of the shelf, opening to reveal the photo of a white woman, her huge siliconed breasts barely covered. The Indian agent suppressed a chuckle.

More shots were fired. Another guard fell. The commander looked over his shoulder at the Indian and raised an eyebrow. Ghazi raised three fingers. The third floor – that's where their target would be be. SEAL

Team Six began climbing up the stairs in single file. The Indian followed.

Inside his bedroom, Osama Bin Laden shook his head. Only a few moments ago, his right-hand man – Abu Ahmed al-Kuwaiti, the fearsome Pashtun who had protected him during the battle of Tora Bora – had picked up his Kalashnikov and rushed to fight the Americans. A brief exchange of fire occurred and Abu Ahmed's war cries eventually fell silent. All of Laden's wives and children, who were huddled together in the room, were weeping inconsolably.

SEAL Team Six entered, barking orders. Amal al-Fatah, the fifth wife, screamed in Arabic and charged at the Americans. She was shot in the foot. Bin Laden looked down, staring at the tiny red dot which had appeared over his chest from the beam of the laser sight mounted over an American rifle. Two bullets hit him in quick succession, the first in the chest and the second above the eye. He fell to the ground. An American shouted over the radio: 'For God and country, Geronimo, Geronimo, Geronimo!'

Ghazi stepped forward and squatted over the body. Swiftly, he collected several DNA samples and placed them in a padded pouch that was secured around his waist. The room was stuffy and reeked of fear and blood. His job was done within minutes and he stood up with a clear thumbs up to the team leader.

'Not outta the fuckin' woods yet, so stop lookin' so happy, Ghazi,' the leader breathed, even as the first screams from outside started. People were gathering and time was running out.

The Americans spared the wailing women and children and those they deemed to be no threat, leaving them behind. They packed Bin Laden in a body bag and carried him away in their helicopter.

A little later, a back-up helicopter arrived to pick up the last of the remaining troops. Ghazi was the last to jump aboard. For the world, he was just another American who had descended on the compound in Abbottabad.

No one had noticed a pair of eyes peering from behind the false wall in Laden's room, taking in every detail about the men who had killed the most wanted terrorist in the world.

1

The snow on the mountains of Kashmir had begun to melt. For Indian troops in the region, it meant preparing for infiltration attempts from across the border. But DIG Ajay Rajvardhan from the NIA was here to stop an enemy from crossing the border into the neighbouring country.

Ajay followed his liaison officer from the Indian army to a waiting jeep. The vehicle sped down the winding road with an amber beacon spinning on its roof. Ajay held tight as it swayed from one turn to another. The thin air carried the scent of flowering gulmohars. He inhaled and cleared his head.

Four hours later, the vehicle slowed down as it neared a nondescript building in the Gurez sector. A sentry in plainclothes allowed the vehicle into the compound. The structure stood in the middle of nowhere and bore no form of identification. No signboard. No nameplates. Anonymity was the key to survival in this beautiful land, which had turned into a hotbed of insurgency. This unmarked building was the zonal headquarters of the Special Operations Group.

Ajay briskly walked into the briefing room. A strike team of seven battle-hardened soldiers had been made available to him. The men were seated in chairs and stood up smartly before Ajay signalled them to be at ease. The lights in the room were switched off and the liaison officer turned on the projector. A disturbing image from Mumbai showed up on the screen: a narrow lane splattered with blood. Tons of dead bodies. Torn limbs.

'Gentlemen,' Ajay said. 'Earlier this year, a high-intensity blast outside a popular bakery in Mumbai killed seventy innocent people.' He paused. 'Maharashtra ATS investigators believe that this blast was planned and executed by Javed Bukhari. Logistical support was provided from across the border.' Another pause. 'Next.'

A bearded young man dressed in combat fatigues showed up on the display screen. Ajay stared hard at the image and gritted his teeth. Javed Bukhari loosely held an AK-47 in his hand. A green headband pushed back his long hair. His posture did not display the discipline of an army regular. Indian agencies had managed to get their hands on many such photographs of Javed in different postures. A video of him playing cricket with his mercenaries had gone viral on WhatsApp. Of course, militants like him gave zero fucks for anonymity. *Good.* Ajay smirked. Javed's thirst for fame on social media would hasten his death.

'Days after the bakery blast, the ATS picked up Javed's presence in Madhya Pradesh,' Ajay said. 'He soon disappeared, only to resurface in Delhi. Before the local agencies could get him, he vanished again. Our intelligence unit has now tracked him to a safe house in Gurez. Javed is waiting to cross the border to perpetual safety. A political career in the long run, perhaps.'

Ajay nodded at the liaison officer. *Click.* A two-storeyed wooden house came up on the screen, and Ajay calmly fielded questions. Yes, the windows were manned by Javed's group. How many men were present in the house? Estimates ranged between five to nine, maybe more. The house was on a hilltop, providing the enemy with the advantage of an elevated position. *Click.* A map demarcating the surrounding landscape showed up on the screen. A red circle marked the house.

'The approach from the south is too steep,' Ajay said. 'Heavy casualties are inevitable if we attack from that direction.'

A team member raised his hand. 'Aerial assault, sir?'

'The roof is covered,' Ajay said. 'A fast-rope insertion can go against us.'

'Rockets?' someone asked. 'We can reduce the house to rubble in no time.'

Ajay shook his head. 'The house belongs to an old woman. Word is that she is being held hostage. We don't want civilians to die.'

'Sir, then how—'

'East,' Ajay said. 'We attack from the east.'

'Sir?' a trooper exclaimed. 'Imagery shows hardly any cover in that direction. We'll be sitting ducks out there!'

Ajay acknowledged the risk with a nod. 'We assault at the break of light.' Then he smiled. 'Now, who do I have to see about getting some good modur pulao for dinner?'

The first azaan of the morning reverberated through the valley. Javed awoke from a disturbed slumber. His hands instinctively grabbed the AK-56 rifle next to his bed. He eased at the sight of his men dutifully manning their positions, chuckling inwardly at the plight of the Indian agencies. Yes, they were tailing him, but he was too smart for them, wasn't he?

One of his comrades brought forth a cup of kahwa. Javed drank in slow gulps. Outside, the sky was still dark.

He spoke in a stern voice. 'The boys are still on the roof?'

'Bilkul, Amir.'

'The En-dians,' Javed said, 'must be crying their hearts out. We hurt them bad, didn't we?'

'Beshaq.'

Javed poked his index finger in his colleague's chest. 'Mumbai! Financial capital of India, huh?' He laughed. 'Their media is breathing fire at me. In newspapers. On television. Perhaps I still appear in their nightmares. Hahaha!'

The fighters in the room laughed along. Javed's laughter grew hysterical. He gulped down the last sip of kahwa and handed the empty cup back to his comrade. At that moment, the guard at the window called out in a rushed tone.

'Jenab,' the guard said. 'I see movement!'

Javed bolted towards the window and snatched the binoculars from the guard's hands. He scanned the area in a grid, moving the lens across, then up and down. When he adjusted the dioptre with his finger, Javed's face turned white. Some kind of abomination – half-man and half-animal – was moving towards them. Javed adjusted the dioptre again and guffawed as the figure became clear to him: a shepherd carrying a goat on his shoulders, with a flock of desi hens tied by their legs in a basket. He was also pulling along another goat.

Javed exhaled a sigh of relief. 'It's only a shepherd.'

The guard aimed his gun. 'Should I blow his head off, jenab?'

'No.' Javed raised his hand in the air. 'We don't fire on our own. The man is only looking to sell his flock. Let him come our way.' He laughed. 'And don't forget – India's most famous agencies have failed to trace me. What harm can one man bring to a great mujahid like me?'

Ajay's muscular shoulders had begun to feel the weight of the Angora goat. The warmth of the animal's belly spread down his neck. Its fur shielded him from the chilly wind. He huffed as he climbed the hilltop, tugging the rope around the neck of the second goat. The animal bleated and followed him like a pet. Ajay shuddered at the thought of the goat deciding not to cooperate. A man from the city, he had little experience of such matters. The animal could blow his cover. And Javed's men would shoot him dead. He had worn a bulletproof vest under the black Pathani suit, but a bullet to the head would mean certain death. 'Good goat,' Ajay whispered. 'Good goat.'

The pathway to the house was lined with tulips and lilies. Ajay's squad was spread behind him. He had ordered them to cover him from a distance, stay behind the boulders or tree trunks, or lie low in the grass until the assault commenced. He whistled the tune of '*Roz roz boz meyn zaar*' into the mic of his voice-operated switch – a signal that he had a visual on the enemy and the terrorists had spotted him. One of them had appeared on the balcony. Ajay sensed his suppressed suspicion from his body language. But he hadn't opened fire yet, which meant the ruse had worked to this point. A rooster crowed from inside his basket.

A few feet away from the entrance, Ajay hunched and lowered the goat off his shoulders. He carried the basket of hens in one hand and walked towards the door. The intricate Persian wooden door remained the only barrier between him and the enemy. Ajay knocked. Seconds later, a militant popped his head out.

Reaching under the layers of his Pathani, Ajay pulled out a 9mm semi-automatic pistol and fired before the militant even realized what was happening. As if on cue, his squad also emerged from their positions and provided him with cover fire.

Ajay kicked the door open. Assault rifles sounded from the floor above. His squad also returned fire. His eyes were set on the staircase to the upper floors.

Suddenly, the door of the room to his left flew open. A terrorist jumped onto Ajay's back. Ajay bent low and threw the terrorist to the ground. His pistol dropped. The terrorist rolled over and pulled out his weapon. While the men were locked in a momentary stare, Ajay quickly pulled a rooster out of his basket and threw it at the militant. The bird flew into the terrorist's face. *Cluck-clack-cluck*. Brown and red feathers floated in the air. Ajay then pulled out a Micro Uzi submachine gun from under his kurta and fired. His attacker dropped dead.

Holding the Uzi's stock to his cheek, Ajay stepped forward. Another militant came sliding down the staircase railing. Ajay caught him at the turn with a burst of fire. He heard his squad closing in on the house. A terrorist fell out the window from the upper floor. His team had scored a kill.

As Ajay rushed past the landing, Javed fired from his assault rifle. Ajay jumped behind the sofa. Javed's last standing guard looked out of the window and was eliminated by Ajay's squad, who had now reached the compound. Javed roared and sprayed a hail of bullets at the sofa. His indiscriminate firing emptied his magazine. As he paused to reload, Ajay jumped forward and shot three bullets into Javed's chest. The militant's rifle fell and his head thudded on the wooden floor. Ajay strode towards him. Javed was trying hard to breathe, but his lips moved. Ajay bent low.

'Y-y-you have merely killed one mujahid.' Javed spat out a mouthful of blood. 'An army of our fighters is waiting at the doors of your cities.' His eyes went blank.

Meanwhile, the squad had reached the upper floor and begun searching the dead bodies. Ajay rifled through the pamphlets and booklets of indoctrination that the militants had carried. The enemies of the nation had managed to brainwash a section of the region into fighting a proxy war. Separatist leaders had played their roles. Local young men were lured to the gun to fight against the Indian armed forces, while the separatists' own children lived in a secure environment in European nations and studied in top universities. Ajay shook his head in disgust. He was crumpling a pamphlet in his palm when an officer walked up to him.

'Sir,' the officer said. 'All bodies accounted for. Control room has been notified.'

'What about the old woman?'

'Sir?'

'The house belonged to an old woman, yes? Where is she?'

'No sign of her, sir. Perhaps these bastards ...'

Just then, a thudding sound was heard. All the officers in the room drew out their guns instinctively.

Ajay held his Uzi low and stepped towards the source of the sound. The sound grew louder and by now, he was able to ascertain that it was coming from underneath the floor. On his orders, one of the troopers pulled off the Kashmiri carpet. Everyone gathered around the trapdoor that had been concealed beneath it.

Ajay signalled with his eyes again. The trooper prepared to lift the trap door. Ajay turned the safety off his gun and aimed in the door's direction. His men followed suit. When the door was finally opened, Ajay saw an old woman staring at him with horrified eyes, her bound legs still in the air after delivering the last thud on the door. Her cries were muffled by the tape tied over her mouth.

The men pulled the old woman out. They removed the tape off her lips and cut open the ropes around her wrist. As soon as the woman was set free, she went about kicking the terrorists' dead bodies. She let loose a barrage of abuses in chaste Kashmiri. 'These are the real enemies,' she screamed. 'Hune! Dogs!'

A trooper tried to restrain the woman, but she rushed towards Ajay. Her eyes were wet as she kissed his hands and continued to speak in Kashmiri, which Ajay couldn't understand. He bemusedly looked at one of the local troopers.

'Sir,' the trooper said. 'She is calling you a saviour sent by Allah.'

'I am honoured that Allah chose me,' he told the woman in broken Kashmiri.

But even as he said it, Javed's final warning was ringing in Ajay's ears. *An army of our fighters is waiting at the doors of your cities.*

2

The Indian Atomic Research Center (IARC) was packed with journalists who had received an invite for a press conference only a few hours ago. More media personnel were jostling at the gates, trying to get inside, even as the security guards did their best to manage the crowd. IARC was India's premier nuclear research facility that had made great achievements for the country.

Mission director, scientist Dhana Swami Chandrashekhar, took a seat in the centre of the dais. His hair was completely grey, but there were no signs of an eccentric genius in his attire. He had cut his hair short and his clothes were crisply ironed. He placed his elbows on the table and leaned forward towards the mic.

Deputy Director Krishnaswamy Ravindran was seated next to his boss. He appeared to be of the same age as Chandrashekhar. He was perspiring down the neck, clearly uncomfortable in the glare of the lights. He picked up a bottle of mineral water from the table and drank in slow gulps.

There was a buzz in the air. Nobody in the media knew about the nature of the mission that the director was leading. The journalists were speculating about the purpose of this media event. The loud whispers came to an abrupt halt as Chandrashekhar began to speak.

'Ladies and gentlemen,' he said with a tinge of pride on his face. 'Buddha has smiled once again.'

A collective gasp ran through the room. Cameras began flashing. The journalists immediately understood Chandrashekhar's reference to Buddha. On 18 May 1974, India had conducted its first nuclear test at an army base in Pokhran, Rajasthan, codenamed 'Smiling Buddha'. This event had largely affected, if not entirely changed, the order of the world as it existed then. It was the first nuclear test by a nation other than the five permanent members of the UN Security Council. The Western powers, who had largely thought of India as a nation of snake charmers, had to stand up and take notice of the country's scientific and military might.

Chandrashekhar looked at the colleagues flanking him and smiled. 'Early this morning, we conducted a successful test of an indigenously developed fusion bomb,' he explained for those who might not have got it. 'Many years of hard work have finally borne fruit.'

'Can you give us more details on the test, sir?' a reporter asked.

'Absolutely,' Chandrashekhar replied. 'This is a thermonuclear weapon with which we have far exceeded previous attempts. In Pokhran-II, our yield was 45 kilotonnes, which was designed to scale for 200 KTs. This time, with a well-researched blueprint, we have achieved capabilities to deliver 600 KTs. In simple terms, we have magnified our nuclear capacity three times.'

Another reporter raised his hand. 'How does this affect our standing in the international community?'

'Our nuclear ambitions have been fuelled by responsibility. But we are also driven by Dr A.P.J. Abdul Kalam, who believed that strength respects strength. His words stand true today more than ever.'

'Did the Western nations have any idea about these tests?'

Chandrashekhar explained that the Indian scientists had calculated the orbits of other nations' satellites, and conducted the movement of their materials in their blind spots. A similar approach had worked during the Pokhran-II tests too. Besides, only a handful of people in India's scientific, defence, political and external affairs establishment had prior information about these developments. This secrecy was necessary for the success of the tests.

'Do you foresee a backlash against this development in the international arena?'

'It would be best if you were to ask the external affairs ministry about that,' Chandrashekhar responded.

The foreign ministry had received a twenty-four-hour advance notice for this test. Their diplomats were already at work to let the world know that India was a responsible nuclear nation which adhered to a no-first-use policy. But like any other self-respecting country, India had the right to pursue avenues for self-defence.

Another reporter stood up and said, 'Sir, a fusion bomb can cause great destruction. To this day, we see that children are born with abnormalities in Japan due to nuclear bombs dropped on Hiroshima and Nagasaki. What is your take on this?'

Chandrashekhar leaned back in his chair. 'I understand your concerns, young lady. But the fact remains that we live in a less-than-ideal world. It is important that we build our strength, even if it is meant to be only a deterrent to the enemies of the nation.' He paused. 'And now we have some visuals to share.'

All heads turned towards the projector screen. The Indian Atomic Research Centre logo appeared on it, with the words 'Atoms in the Service of the Nation' in English and Devanagari script. Then the image shifted to the deserts of Jaisalmer in Rajasthan, where the Pokhran Test Range was located. The entire media contingent looked on in awe as the desert shook under the impact of the bomb. Plumes of dust blew in the air. A helicopter surveyed the crater created by the detonation. Then a summary graph of the results was put up.

As the conference neared to an end, every person in the room clapped. People rushed to congratulate Chandrashekhar.

Foreign news channels had already picked up the story by the time the media filed out of the conference room, and it had created quite a ripple across the world, especially in Southeast Asia. Indian news channels were running amok with headlines like '*Thar Thar Kapa Pakistan*' (Pakistan is shivering in fear). The Rashtrapati Bhavan and Prime Minister's Office extended their heartiest congratulations to Chandrashekhar and his team. Within a few hours, the IARC was buzzing with talk about Chandrashekhar being in line for the Padma Shri.

Chandrashekhar's staff lined up and clapped as he exited the building. Media persons accosted him as he went towards his car, while his security cleared a path. Cameras flashed at the car's tinted windows as he got in. He had become a celebrity overnight.

All of the IARC's staff went home that evening eagerly anticipating the detailed media coverage of their runaway success. Televisions were switched on well before the 9 p.m. bulletin. The more tech savvy ran online searches and bookmarked any web pages with news articles about the feat. Everyone eagerly waited to see the next day's newspapers.

Which is why it came as a rude shock to those who had missed the midnight news when the next morning, every news channel's ticker announced, 'Scientist D. Chandrashekhar found hung to death!'

3

Joint Commissioner of Police (Crime) Sagar Pratap was no stranger to dead bodies. His eyes followed the coir rope from the centre of the ceiling fan to the knot around Chandrashekhar's neck. Pratap stroked his bushy moustache. The victim showed no signs of life. Resuscitation would not help. There was no haste to get him to a hospital. But an ambulance was waiting downstairs, and a huge crowd had already gathered around it.

Hues of dark blue had formed over Chandrashekhar's tongue, which was stretching out of his mouth. He was thin and short; Pratap estimated his weight to be around sixty-five kilogrammes. The spick-and-span condition of the house, the lined arrangement of the pillows on the sofa and the neatly stacked issues of the *Scientific Indian* magazine on the coffee table bore grave testimony to the orderliness of the man who was no more. Even in death, D. Chandrashekhar had followed the same methodical approach that had been the hallmark of his scientific expeditions.

Staff from the forensics department were finishing their last set of photographs. Yellow tape with clear warnings had sealed off the room. The victim was wearing a crisply ironed white shirt and grey trousers. Pratap opened the cupboard and saw stacks of identical sets. Perhaps Chandrashekhar's simplicity stemmed from his genius.

A wooden chair was upturned near his drooping legs. He'd kicked the chair underneath with all his strength. Rigor mortis had set in and his muscles had stiffened. The doors and windows showed no signs of forced entry, and the room did not show any signs of struggle.

'Who found the body?' Pratap asked, still looking at the macabre scene.

One of the constables behind him answered, 'His team tried reaching him late last night, sir, because the PMO asked for some information. He would normally never ignore work calls, or if he missed one, would call back promptly. So, when the calls went unanswered for a few hours, someone from the team drove down.

When no one opened the door, they broke it down and found the body.'

Pratap turned around.

'Cut the rope above the knot,' he said. 'Get him down.'

Two paunchy constables and a helper brought down the body with relative ease. Pratap knew it was an important piece of evidence. He studied the frail scientist and found no external injury marks. The victim's shirt smelled of Scotch, and it looked like he'd had one drink too many, to the point of spilling it all over his clothes.

The man had been the toast of the media just twenty-four hours ago. But Pratap's investigation revealed that Chandrashekhar was also seeing a therapist in Kemps Corner for clinical depression.

Pratap sighed. Yet another brilliant mind had fallen, he thought. Snapping on a pair of latex gloves, he squatted close to Chandrashekhar's body and began to examine it. He held the victim's hand in his own.

'No scrapings under the fingernails,' he announced.

A constable took notes in a red diary. Pratap studied the ligature marks around the victim's neck. The sharp lines seemed to match the thickness of the coir rope. Fibres from the rope had stuck on to the victim's neck. Pratap held Chandrashekhar's chin and turned it from one side to another. He unbuttoned the shirt for a closer look.

'No signs of external injuries,' he said.

But he had to find a motive, for a death like this demanded one. He checked the pockets of Chandrashekhar's trousers. He found a wallet which contained a decent amount of cash and the scientist's identification card from the IARC.

'There was a note?' he asked, directing the question at no one in particular.

One of the forensic technicians stepped forward and the late scientist's suicide note made its way from one gloved hand to another.

It simply said:

Is any cause worth bringing death upon a million lives?

Chandrashekhar's empirical compass seemed to have malfunctioned under ethical pressure. His body would soon begin to decompose. Pratap knew the onset of that stench.

There was work to be done. The investigation demanded that they speak to the neighbours, the watchman, the maid, the milkman, the victim's colleagues and whoever else they could lay their hands upon.

'Okay,' he said. 'Send the body for a postmortem.'

The Police Commissionerate at Crawford Market stood sturdy in the heart of the city. Commissioner Neeraj Kumar had taken over this assignment in the sunset of a distinguished career. A product of the Indian Police Service (IPS), he had been an English literature professor at a well-known university before securing an AIR (All India Rank) of thirty-seven in the Civil Service Examination of 1990. He had chosen the crispness of the khaki over the lure of babudom.

The advent of his career coincided with his professional handling of communally charged situations in the early '90s. Even in his initial years, he had shown a flair for words and an appetite for risk, which had strengthened his candidature for the top job after decades of service.

The bakery blast by terrorist Javed Bukhari had caused a 'routine transfer' of the previous commissioner to the State Police Housing and Welfare Department. Kumar's impeccable track record had prevailed over the other contenders to the post. And he had not failed his bosses. The backlash from the bakery blast had eased after Javed's encounter by the NIA.

Now, CP Kumar sat comfortably in his chair, flipping over a page from the pale blue file Pratap had just handed over. He skimmed through the pages, pausing at certain points with an expression of surprise.

'What did Chandrashekhar's therapist have to say?' Kumar asked.

'Sir.' Pratap nodded. 'The victim was prescribed a high dose of tricyclic antidepressants. Elavil, to be precise.'

Kumar moved forward two pages. 'What about his colleagues?'

'Our man was a loner in life and death. His colleague Mr Ravindran had kind words to say about his boss. The victim was professional in his interactions at the workplace, but never discussed personal matters. He and his wife had separated in the first year of their marriage. He never remarried. No one knew if he had had any affairs in the interim.'

'What about his neighbours?'

'One of them had invited him to lunch. He politely accepted but never turned up and switched off his phone on the day too. He was quite an anti-social old man. He'd nailed wooden planks to his windows because the kids in the colony played cricket in the compound and it disturbed his afternoon nap. Overall, he was perceived as a person who did not want to be disturbed and everyone left him alone.'

'Known enemies? Ancestral property disputes?'

'None, sir.'

'Anyone who had a word of praise for him?'

'Everyone,' Pratap said. 'Even the watchman, whom Mr Chandrashekhar paid thrice the usual rate for washing his Maruti Zen every day, could not stop singing his paeans.'

Kumar was surprised. Chandrashekhar could have easily afforded a new car, but perhaps the scientist had other priorities.

The telephone on Kumar's desk rang. The constable sitting at the reception had called.

'Send them in,' Kumar said on the phone and turned back to Pratap. 'New Delhi is interested in this case, Pratap. A team from the NIA is here.'

At that moment, Pratap could see that Kumar was as displeased as him about a central agency wanting to hog the limelight yet again in a crucial case. It happened all the time and he was tired of it. Nevertheless, he turned his neck at the approaching sound of leather shoes and high heels.

The NIA team consisted of a woman in her mid-forties, wearing a crisp Paithani saree, and a man in his mid-thirties. Kumar stood up to greet them and Pratap followed suit. He was, after all, his boss's man.

The woman introduced herself as Swati Gokhale, deputy director with the NIA, and firmly shook hands with Kumar and Pratap. She pointed at the male officer.

'This is DIG Ajay Rajvardhan,' she said.

'Oh, yes,' Pratap said. 'Mr James Bond has been all over the papers recently for the Javed Bukhari encounter. The approach was quite risky, I must say.'

Ajay smirked at the underhanded compliment. 'We suffered no casualties during the encounter. But thank you.'

'Of course,' Kumar said. He could recognize the start of a rivalry when he saw one. Which was a tad surprising, as Pratap was a rank senior to Ajay.

Swati and Ajay settled into two empty chairs. Pratap moved his chair slightly to create some space between himself and the NIA officers.

'Can you brief us on the case, JCP Pratap?' Ajay said.

'Absolutely,' Pratap said. 'A request from a super-agent and super-spy has to be acceded to.'

Pratap reluctantly briefed the team about Chandrashekhar's death. Ajay heard him out patiently, and many questions began brewing in his mind. He had picked up the sarcasm dripping from Pratap's tone. He knew he would have to find the answers quickly, before the professional rivalry affected the investigation.

Ajay listened quietly, didn't take any notes and asked very few questions.

But by the time the briefing was done, he was feeling an itch in his brain. Already, it was working overtime to connect the dots that only he could see. There was one thing he was already quite certain about.

This was not a suicide.

4

The special court was jam-packed. A posse of policemen had accompanied Nazneen Dharker. She had been arrested by the state police on charges of terrorism, based on intel passed by the NIA. Her lawyer had filed for bail, citing wrongful custody. Ajay had reluctantly come to the court to represent his organization. He hated attending court hearings, even though he respected them. He took a seat in the gallery strategically close to the public prosecutor.

Uttam Nigam, the public prosecutor for the case, looked over his shoulder and rolled his eyes as Ajay settled into the wooden bench just as the proceedings were to start. As the judge began, Ajay could not help but wonder which lawyer had picked up Nazneen's case. Lawyers in the city had become increasingly hesitant about defending terror-related cases.

As the defence lawyer arrived, Ajay watched her curiously. She carried herself well, exuded confidence and didn't seem to be very well-known. Hardly three or four other lawyers exchanged nods with her. New to the city, Ajay deduced.

He was aware of a feeling of childish excitement, tinged with the antagonism any cop feels towards a defence lawyer.

Nigam was a wily old fox. He would tangle this young lady in a web of legal holds, which he had mastered over three decades. This hearing was the proverbial David against Goliath, but Ajay was sure that his Goliath would crush the supposed David in no time. Which meant that Ajay could return to work soon instead of spending his time in a courtroom.

Nigam began in his usual style, opening with a Sanskrit shloka about the collective conscience of the society, which had been shaken by recent acts of terror. He put forth a solid argument. The crowd and even the judge appeared mesmerized by his grip on the case. The accused stood in the wooden box with her head lowered. Her shoulders sagged as Nigam pounded on. The defence lawyer narrowed her eyes and leaned forward.

Nigam pointed a finger at Nazneen. 'This woman,' he said, 'has been making calls to numbers across the border. We have already submitted her call records at the first remand hearing after her arrest. We suspect she had prior knowledge of the bakery blasts, which rocked the city a few months ago. The police need more time to investigate this angle. Hence, we are requesting an extension of her police custody.'

The judge called for the defence to present their case. 'Where is the defence attorney?' he asked.

The lady lawyer whom Ajay had been watching intently stood up. 'Here, Your Honour,' she said. 'Advocate Asiya Khan, LLB.'

Ajay repeated the name in his head. *Asiya.*

'Proceed,' the judge said.

'Your Honour,' Asiya said. 'The police are demanding an extension of custody even though seven days of remand have failed to produce absolutely anything except circumstantial evidence.'

Nigam interjected. 'My young colleague,' he said patronizingly, 'seems to forget that complex investigations take time. We have sent a letter rogatory to the email provider for the accused. The company is based in Silicon Valley and has not responded so far. And then there is the question of the phone calls to Pakistan.'

'In that case,' Asiya retorted, 'the constitutional rights of the accused must be restored until she is proven guilty.'

'What about the calls she made to her handlers?' Nigam asked.

'The learned counsel is speculating,' Asiya said.

'An NIA investigation has found calls made from her number to Karachi,' Nigam said. 'I fail to see how that amounts to speculation.'

'I am aware of the NIA's involvement. In fact, I am even aware that the NIA officer who led the probe is present in court today.' Asiya cast a sharp look in Ajay's direction.

Ajay was taken aback. That did not sound good at all.

Asiya pulled out a cellphone from her pocket and asked the judge for permission to make a demonstration.

'Granted,' the judge said.

'Technological advancements have their own flaws,' Asiya said. 'It is fairly easy for a technologically adept criminal to take control of someone else's phone and make calls even from a remote location.' She pressed a few buttons on her phone. Her phone began to ring as if she had received a call. 'As you can see, a number starting 98207 is calling my phone right now.' She rattled off the entire number to the court. 'May I know if this number belongs to someone present in the court?'

Nigam jumped out of his seat.

'I don't know what game you're playing, young lady …'

'If it may please the court,' Asiya cut in calmly, 'this number belongs to my learned senior colleague here.'

For the first time in maybe a decade, or even two, Nigam had no retort.

'And thus,' Asiya said, 'I could have made a call to Islamabad or Karachi and claimed that the learned public prosecutor should be put behind bars.'

Utter silence in the court was followed by murmurs and hushed chaos. Nigam stood where he was, staring daggers at Asiya.

His brain worked furiously, trying to find a loophole. But the few minor defeats, which he had tasted in his long career, had taught him that this battle was lost already. He tried to keep a straight face, but the fact that a young *female* lawyer had outsmarted him had punctured his ego.

'And the honourable Supreme Court has dictated multiple times that bail should be the norm instead of jail,' Asiya continued. 'I pray to the court that this norm is upheld and my client's bail is approved.'

Ajay's eyes were fixated on Asiya's sharp movements as the judge approved the bail, subject to conditions that the accused would not travel out of the city and would mark her presence at the local police station at least twice in a calendar month. A fuming Nigam left the court in a huff. The media went into a total frenzy. They started hounding Asiya for a byte, but she just brushed past them into the canteen meant only for lawyers and other officials.

Ajay followed her and slid into the seat across from her.

'If I may take just one second of your time …' he said.

'You're the investigating officer of the case against my client, so ideally, no, you may not,' she said, but she was grinning. The walls of this canteen had seen the bitterest of adversaries share a meal after battling it out in the courtroom.

Ajay returned the grin.

'I will deny this if you ever quote me,' he said, leaning a little closer and lowering his voice, 'but if you agree, I'd like to buy you coffee, simply for that amazing show you put on in court today.'

Asiya's grin widened.

'You want to treat me to coffee because I tore your case apart?'

'Quite the contrary,' Ajay replied. 'I was content to let the bail hearings rest on call records, so that we could save the rest for the trial stage. Now I get to break out the big guns.'

Asiya's smile remained.

'You don't have any big guns, Mr Ajay.'

'We'll see at the next hearing, Ms Asiya.'

There was a pause. Ajay leaned in even closer.

'Also,' he said, 'like we do with any emerging technology, we've been quietly monitoring scores of people who've been using these call-spoofing programmes for nefarious purposes. Thanks to you, the cat is now out of the bag.'

'Umm ... should I be apologizing?'

'Not really. I texted all my officers to move the minute you pulled that stunt in court. They're raiding seven locations as we speak. We're having a big press conference in the evening AND the government is finally deeming the apps illegal. So thanks for that.'

Ajay stood up and walked away, leaving Asiya staring after him.

5

Ajay waited outside Commissioner Kumar's cabin, a laptop bag slung over his shoulder. A constable, who was designated as the stick-walker, was standing at attention by the door. Mumbai police tradition dictated that whenever the commissioner arrived at the office, four armed sentries would give him a guard of honour, then the stick-walker would guide the CP to his cabin on the first floor. At the end of the shift, another stick-walker would guide the commissioner back to his official vehicle.

The authorities had also installed a mirror near the door for visitors to spruce themselves up before meeting the CP. As Ajay was adjusting his shirt collar, the thought of Asiya grazed his mind. Her kohl-laden eyes, which he had been fixated upon in the court, were imprinted on his mind.

His recent investigations had thrown up an interesting development, which warranted a discussion with the CP. As he was called into the office, he quickly ran his fingers through his hair and rushed inside. The policemen exchanged salutations.

With a disarming smile, the CP gestured at Ajay to take a seat and ordered his reception to send in a cup of coffee. Ajay wasn't surprised. Clearly, Kumar had conducted his due diligence and even knew that Ajay preferred coffee over tea. On the surface, the Mumbai police and the NIA were on the same side. But underneath, the currents of interagency rivalry were heavily at play. Ajay had grown up in Mumbai, but he was currently on deputation to the NIA. His loyalties were firmly with Delhi. Kumar would be well aware of this fact.

The two cops were still engaged in small talk when the orderly arrived with the tray. The moment he left, Kumar got down to business.

'So, what happened at the bail hearing?' he asked. 'Nigam is still fuming?'

'Nazneen's lawyer was on top of her game,' Ajay said. 'So yes, Nigam threw a fit about it when I met him at his office.'

'Asiya may have saved Nazneen for now,' Kumar said. 'But we worked on the NIA's lead along with the ATS, Ajay. Our investigations do not give a clean chit to Nazneen either. She seems to be a part of a larger design.'

'What are you suggesting, sir?'

'An anarchist group,' Kumar said. 'Something like a sleeper cell. I am not sure yet. Why don't you put a tail on her?' He paused. 'Pratap can arrange local resources for this task. I can talk to the ATS.'

'Thank you, sir, but I'll figure something out on that front,' Ajay said. 'However, your attention is requested on an important angle related to Chandrashekhar's death.'

Kumar leaned forward, suddenly interested. He had not expected this.

Ajay pulled his laptop out of the bag. He used a dongle to connect to the internet. Using a virtual private network, he established a secure connection to the NIA's network. A black-and-green screen showed up. He entered his credentials and accessed a confidential document. On the first slide, there was a photograph of a bald man in a lab coat, with text around it. Some keywords were highlighted.

Ajay cleared his throat. 'The person on the screen is Manoj Sharma, an experienced engineer, who was last posted with the Defence Research Corporation of India (DRCI), based in Bengaluru. In mid-2017, a railway guard was checking the fish plates along Bengaluru City Railway Station when he noticed an immobile body on the tracks. An incoming freight train was about to pass on its regular schedule. The alert guard communicated with the railway traffic controller and the train was stopped just before it was about to run over the body.' He paused. 'Later, at a government hospital, the victim was identified as Manoj Sharma. He'd been dead long before his body was moved to the railway tracks. Eventually, investigations hit a dead end and the case was closed as an accidental death.'

'So what's the catch?' Kumar asked.

'In 2016, Dr Sharma had spent time at the Indian Atomic Research Centre. He was a part of the design team working under Mr Chandrashekhar, who was then laying the foundations of "Operation Trishul", the codename for developing this fusion bomb.'

'Interesting.' Kumar rested his chin on his thumbs and leaned forward. 'Very interesting.'

Ajay clicked 'next'. Another photograph showed up. The man on the screen was in his fifties and wearing golden-framed spectacles. 'This is Dr Narasimha Reddy. In 2018, he opted for voluntary retirement from the Directorate of Atomic Energy. Post retirement, he moved to his bungalow on the outskirts of Hyderabad.

Later that year, Dr Reddy drowned in his swimming pool.' Ajay paused. 'But here's the surprising fact: Dr Reddy was a gold medallist in swimming during his pre-university days. Like Sharma and Chandrashekhar, he was also a loner. High levels of alcohol found in his bloodstream supposedly caused him to drown.'

'And Dr Reddy spent time with IARC too?'

'Precisely,' Ajay said. 'Reddy worked with Chandrashekhar in 2017 on the reactor for Operation Trishul. Chandrashekhar's blood sample, like Reddy's, also showed unusually high alcohol levels.'

'So the three deaths are connected to Operation Trishul?'

'Sir, the similarities cannot be ignored. Chandrashekhar was a marked man even before his death. This CCTV footage is the evidence.'

Ajay played a video file on his laptop. The footage had been collected from a closed-circuit camera near Chandrashekhar's home. A date of around eight months prior appeared at the bottom right of the screen. The footage was dark and grainy, given the late hour of the night it was captured on. A few vehicles were parked under a 'No Parking' sign. Chandrashekhar appeared on the screen, crossing a lonely street near his home. Another camera captured him entering a 24/7 pharmacy. A few minutes later, Chandrashekhar emerged from the shop. He was crossing back when a black sedan with tinted windows came speeding down the road. The car was about to mow him down when he jumped at the last moment and saved his life.

'Sir,' Ajay said. 'A random drunkard may have been behind the wheel, but it could also be the first concerted attempt on Chandrashekhar's life. He probably did not report it, thinking that the incident was a one-off.'

'I'm sure you checked the sedan's number plate,' Kumar said.

'The car was reported stolen months before this incident,' Ajay replied. 'I checked on the complainant. The owner is a college professor from Andheri. Her background checks show no cause for suspicion.'

'Okay,' Kumar said. 'But if your hunch is true, we have a big problem on our hands.'

'Yes, sir.' Ajay paused. 'My theory is that Sharma's, Reddy's and Chandrashekhar's deaths are the handiwork of the same person.' Another pause. 'Chandrashekhar's murder is the third act of a serial killer who is eliminating India's nuclear scientists, one by one.'

6

The 'Perfect Cut' boutique shop signboard in Kurla was glowing on and off at regular intervals. Customers would throng the shop during the day, but now, at midnight, it was closed for business. Its top floor had a designer feel to it with elegant yellow lighting and a plaster of Paris ceiling. Black mannequins adorned in white chikankari-embroidered dresses posed elegantly. Exquisite pashminas, shahtoosh and namdas materials from Kashmir were its USP.

In the shop's basement, accessible only by a concealed entrance, Nazneen sat cross-legged on the floor. Another woman in her fifties, Hafsa Begum, was sitting on the sofa. Tears streamed down Nazneen's eyes as she held Hafsa's legs and begged for mercy.

'You were careless,' Hafsa said. 'I should have let you rot in jail!'

'Forgive me, Hafsa Bi.'

'I should have never trusted you,' Hafsa thundered. 'You almost blew our cover.'

This shop was one of the many fronts used by the 'Khwaharan-e-Millat', a sisterhood which had spread its tentacles in India with the sole aim of destabilizing the nation. Hafsa was at the apex of this movement.

The events leading to Nazneen's arrest had originated with an indiscreet phone call. The Data Intelligence Unit of the NIA would routinely scan millions of telephone call records across the country for suspicious calls using artificial intelligence. In this data mining exercise, a handful of numbers were flagged as suspect, based on the locations with which they were communicating and the frequency and duration of the calls. Nazneen had called a contact of the 'Khwaharan-e-Millat' who was currently operating across the border without taking the necessary precautions. Based on this intel from the NIA, the Maharashtra Anti-Terrorism Squad had put her number under surveillance.

Even prior to her arrest, Nazneen had received a verbal lashing from Hafsa after her indiscretion was discovered. She took due care not to repeat the same mistake. However, the ATS grew tired of the waiting game and decided to arrest her, with the hope that it would gather more evidence against her later. But using the layers of social connections established by Hafsa Begum over the years, legal help had been arranged.

'I will repay this debt with my life,' Nazneen declared, kissing Hafsa's hands.

At this, Hafsa's fury mellowed and she placed her palm on Nazneen's head. 'My child, your life is precious for our goal.'

Hafsa switched on a news channel on the television. The prime-time debate was about to begin. Chandrashekhar's death was being covered by the media round the clock and was the subject of discussion here as well.

The opening visual of the news debate was a badly photoshopped picture of Chandrashekhar in a lab coat with a rope around his neck. The media tended to overdramatize deaths.

Hafsa chuckled and increased the volume. The male anchor was dressed in a black suit and red tie. In an overdramatic manner, he revealed that Chandrashekhar's death was being investigated by the National Investigation Agency. Ajay's photo was displayed. Nazneen flew into a rage at the mere sight of his face.

'This bastard was responsible for my arrest,' Nazneen said.

'I'm aware,' Hafsa replied. 'He has caused me a lot of grief too. The police had never seen my face until Javed Bukhari was encountered in Kashmir. The bakery blasts got to Javed's head. He was under strict orders not to establish any contact, but the khabees actually had the gall to come to my house for a pit stop before crossing the border. Had I not portrayed myself as a hostage, I too would be sleeping in my grave like Javed right now.'

Nazneen looked at Hafsa in awe.

However, Javed's encounter had led to Hafsa becoming a person of interest for the authorities. To continue laying low, she moved out of Kashmir on the pretext that she feared the *terrorists* would seek revenge from her for Javed's killing. Mumbai was the perfect destination. The K-e-M network in the city would provide refuge and she could also keep a close eye on Ajay.

'But what are we going to do about this policewala?' Nazneen asked.

Hafsa stared at Ajay's photograph. She dipped her hand into a box of clothes on a table nearby and pulled out a Russian Makarov pistol. Then she closed an eye and aimed the gun at Ajay's face.

'My child,' Hafsa said. 'We are already making arrangements. Wait and watch.'

7

In the seventh-floor NIA office at Cumbala Hill, Ajay leaned back in his chair and stared at the ceiling. For two and a half hours, he'd been submerged in a chart he had drawn to analyse the link between the death of the three scientists. His mind was now tired and hazy. He then got up and opened the window to breathe in some fresh air.

Outside, the many high-rises peaked towards the Mumbai skyline. Tall mobile towers lined the terraces. Warning lights for aeroplanes blinked in red against the dark grey clouds. Ajay had felt a certain despondency in this city after his mother had passed away many years ago in their small apartment in Colaba. It was one of the reasons why he had moved to Delhi, and he wanted to get back to the capital now, even though its air pollution levels were poisonous for his lungs. Somehow, he found that notion much more acceptable than being distraught remembering his mother.

The phone on his desk rang.

'Sir,' the constable at the reception said. 'A lawyer is here to meet you.'

'Is this by appointment?' he said tersely.

'I tried explaining to her, sir,' the constable said. 'But she is adamant.'

'Her?' The aggression in Ajay's voice toned down. 'What is *her* ... the lawyer's name?'

The constable placed a hand over the receiver and Ajay heard him ask the visitor in a rather courteous voice: *'Naav kay apla?'*

Ajay recognized the voice even before he heard the name. He contained the excitement in his voice and ordered the constable to allow the visitor through, with due respect. Soon enough, the door opened with a click.

Asiya was wearing a white dress with a black dupatta. Light from the corridor was shining directly behind her. His heart thumped like he was back in college, but he quickly regained his composure and stood up to greet her. She responded to his gentle smile with the forced seriousness of a lawyer. With each step she took, the tinkle of her anklets echoed in his ears. He pulled out a chair for her and retreated to the other side of the table. She took her seat, and the subtle scent of her perfume infused his heart with an emotion of such complexity that he feared it might be love after all.

Asiya was caught off-guard, as she had expected a rather hostile reception. She shifted in her chair a few times. Filigree diamond studs were shining in her earlobes. She moved a strand of hair across her forehead with her long, slender fingers.

Ajay asked for her choice of hot beverage but she refused – rather curtly, he thought. Then she opened the file which she was carrying and placed it on the table. It was time for business and she put on her best poker face.

'You've secured bail for your client already,' Ajay said. 'How can I help you now?'

'Countless others like Nazneen, from my community, are still rotting in jail.'

'And there are reasons behind their arrest.'

'It stands to logic that a government servant would have a lot of faith in charges which are slapped by his government against members of a certain community,' Asiya said. 'Admit it or not, the religion of my clients is the only reason for their prolonged detention.'

She jerked her arm. Ajay noticed that her triceps were in perfect shape. He was taken aback by her offensive, though, as Asiya went on with her impassioned tirade against the system.

She explained that a few months ago, the police had picked up thirty-five-year-old Iqbal Qureishi from Aurangabad on mere suspicion of terror links. His wife had been unable to secure bail for him because she could not afford a good lawyer. In Mumbra, nineteen-year-old Asif Shaikh was arrested for exchanging messages with a social media account, which was later discovered to be operating from beyond the border. Common sense dictated that this account was a catfish – a man posing as a woman – and had enticed Asif's raging hormones into a discussion about ISIS. But now Asif was languishing in jail, even when his messages to the catfish had showed no signs of any radical intentions. Lastly, in the Konkan region, the police had arrested Imran Parkar, who was also struggling for bail, despite the flimsy evidence that had been allegedly planted on him.

'I've followed these three cases closely,' Asiya concluded. 'These men deserve bail. And the orders to oppose the bail, I have been told, originate from the NIA.'

Ajay picked up the file and turned over the pages. 'The NIA officer who was in charge before me had ordered these arrests,' he said. 'I will go through their files and see what I can do.'

'That sounds perfunctory.' Asiya extended her hand to take the file back. 'For the state, the lives of these innocent people are meaningless. But every day I see men and women from our community being picked up on flimsy grounds. They get locked up for years and their cases drag on for eternity. Even if they are acquitted in the end, their families are shattered. Is this justice?'

Ajay tried to remain disconnected and made a few mental calculations. 'We can work out something specific for these three men,' he said. 'But only if you will assist the department in a matter of high confidentiality. The department won't oppose the bail of your clients if you work with us. You have my word on that.'

'Bail is a legal remedy provided by the court.' Asiya placed her palms on the table and stood. 'I will not negotiate over the lives of innocents.'

Ajay placed his visiting card on the table. 'Call me if you change your mind.'

Asiya was now locked in a momentary stare down with Ajay. His guard lowered at the sight of her hazel-brown eyes. But he jammed the emotion from showing on his face.

Asiya spun around and thumped her way towards the door. She held the door ajar for a moment. He kept his gaze on her back. Then she turned and walked back to the desk and collected Ajay's contact card from the table. She stormed out again and slammed the door behind her. Ajay grinned. He had planted the seed in her mind. Now he would wait to see if it bore fruit.

Back home, Ajay sat at the dining table with little appetite. His orderly served him a plate of curd and rice. This was his comfort food, and he found solace in mixing grains of rice with chunks of curd using his fingers. Above, the fan twirled.

Asiya had left an imprint on his mind. He did not want to give her more reasons to hate him. She was angry with the system. And he was part of the system she hated.

Halfway into the meal, he gulped down a glass of water and went to wash his hands, while the orderly picked up the unfinished plate with a shake of his head. He then retired to his bedroom and changed into a loose kurta and white pyjama. He sat cross-legged on his bed. Another thought of his mother shoved him further into loneliness. He switched off the lights and closed his eyes, but couldn't sleep. A speeding car drove through the street below.

His thoughts went to Asiya again. He'd had his share of relationships, but he'd never felt this kind of longing before. He wanted to be in Asiya's company all the time.

His phone lit up. The notifications showed that he had received an instant message from an unknown number. He enlarged the sender's display picture. It was Asiya, holding a bouquet of white lilies. She was leaning back and smiling, with her hair covering part of her face.

The message read: *Awake?*

Yes, he responded.

Sorry for what happened in the evening. Can we meet tomorrow?

Sure. How about before noon? At my office?

Not possible. Hearing at the Bandra court. How about Romano Cafe at Carter Road in the evening?

Ajay started typing an answer, but he found that saying yes was harder than he thought it would have been. Another message popped up on his screen.

Cops are supposed to show some urgency to late-night messages, no? ;-)

He smiled and typed: *Okay. 1800 hours?*

Ajay bit his tongue lightly as soon as he sent the message. Officers always referred to the time as per the twenty-four-hour clock.

Asiya, however, seemed to be used to this, maybe because she spent most of her time interacting with cops.

Done, she replied. *I'll be waiting. Goodnight.*

She went offline even as Ajay was typing his goodbye. He deleted the message and placed the phone on the dressing table next to the bed. He recited a prayer which his amme had taught him. In his mind, he could hear it in her voice. Now his eyes closed.

Some distance apart, in Byculla, Asiya was thinking about Ajay too. Sure, he had been polite and courteous to her. Also, she could see that he was smitten with her. She smiled. He wasn't that bad-looking either. She allowed herself a giggle. But amidst all this, she was also thinking about the offer Ajay had made for the bail of her three clients. What kind of deal did he want to strike with her?

8

The next morning, Ajay drove to Chandrashekhar's apartment in the IARC officers' quarters, accompanied by two constables. The building was located on the outskirts of the city, close to the atomic centre. Ajay took the elevator to Chandrashekhar's floor. The door of the flat had been sealed by the police.

'Open it,' Ajay said.

The constables broke the seal and opened the door. Ajay stepped into the house. A repugnant but familiar stench of death wafted through the air. He checked the wooden frame for signs of chipping. He ran his hand over the door to check for recent repairs or fresh coats of paint. There were none. Pratap was right. There were no signs of forced entry. The tick-tock of the wall clock sounded clear in the silence. Perhaps Chandrashekhar had known his killer. Had the hunter and the hunted entered the house together?

Pratap had done a decent job in preserving the scene of crime. Much of the house was undisturbed since his investigation. It meant that no other agencies had entered the premises. *Good.* Ajay felt better knowing that the scene had not been contaminated.

He put on a pair of white gloves and entered Chandrashekhar's bedroom. His objective today was to conduct a blood-spatter analysis, which could be used to detect traces of blood in the room. He hung a dual-band UV and infrared camera around his neck. On his signal, the constables closed the door and pulled the curtains tight. The room went dark. Ajay's eyes fluttered. He switched on the camera and scanned the room for blood. The camera could identify patterns in which different substrates reflected and absorbed ultraviolet and infrared illumination in different quantities. He could see no signs of blood. Dead end.

On the white bedsheet, he could see traces of body fluids. Sweat. Semen. Was this a crime of passion? He didn't know yet. He rummaged through the drawer in the wardrobe. A half-empty packet of condoms was hidden under a notepad. The notepad contained a lot of handwritten text and Ajay clicked photographs of a few pages where Chandrashekhar's handwriting was clear. Then he pulled out his cellphone and called up a contact in the Document Analysis Unit of the NIA.

'I am sending two handwriting samples for comparison,' he said.

'Sure. Please submit the physical samples today and we'll send the reports in two weeks,' the bored-sounding analyst replied.

'If I don't get the reports in two hours,' Ajay answered, 'I will personally ensure your transfer to a remote corner of the country.'

He disconnected the call before the analyst had any time to react. Then he picked up the packet of condoms, using a pair of tweezers, and packed it as evidence.

Ajay retreated to the living room. From the photographs of the crime scene clicked by Pratap's team, he identified the stool, which Chandrashekhar had apparently kicked away. Ajay placed the same stool underneath the fan again. He picked up a stuffed dummy, weighing as much as Chandrashekhar, which the constables had brought along.

Climbing up on the stool, he tied the rope, with a noose already at its end, around the ceiling fan and then tried slipping the noose around the dummy's neck. But the stool was too small for him to complete the act while supporting the dummy's weight.

He ordered the constables to search the house for something heavier than the stool, and the men found a metal ladder in the drying area. Ajay repeated the test with the ladder and found some success in manoeuvring the body into the position in which it was found. The ladder's rungs bore footmarks in the accumulated dust. Their size did not seem to match Chandrashekhar's foot size. Ajay photographed the marks.

And then Ajay found something stuck in the lower rungs. He looked closely. A broken fingernail. He pulled out the nail with tweezers and placed it in a plastic pouch. Ajay smiled. He loved being right.

Pratap was sitting in his cabin at the commissionerate and browsing through a file when he was summoned to Kumar's cabin. When he entered the room, he found Ajay already seated there. The commissioner asked Pratap to also take a seat. His face appeared rather grim.

'Pratap,' Kumar said, 'a good cop is one who never gets complacent.' He paused. Pratap said nothing, but experience had taught him that whenever your senior begins the conversation on a philosophical note, it never bodes well for you.

'Are you sure that Chandrashekhar committed suicide?' Kumar asked.

'Absolutely, sir,' Pratap said. 'I found a suicide note in the room. The lesion marks on the victim's neck matched the coir rope wrapped around it. At the time of death, the victim was under the influence of alcohol. He was also consulting a top therapist in south Mumbai. I don't see another angle to this case, sir.'

Kumar pointed towards Ajay. 'The NIA has a different view.'

Pratap scoffed. 'My investigation is thorough, sir.'

Kumar gave Ajay the go-ahead to explain his position. Ajay proceeded to tear Pratap's theory apart, point by point.

The first piece which he had analysed was the suicide note. Firstly, Ajay explained, it was not an elaborate note but a single line: *Is any cause worth bringing death upon a million lives?* This looked like a philosopher's musing. And the Document Analysis Unit of the NIA had confirmed that even though the handwriting sample from the suicide note closely resembled the handwriting from the notepad which Ajay had sent across, the samples were *not* an exact match. 'There's a difference in the cross over the t's,' Ajay said and showed the report in which the differences were circled in red ink.'

'What about the lesion marks?' Pratap asked.

'Forensics is still trying to figure out if the lesions are forced or voluntary. Even if the marks are voluntary, we cannot rule out a hangman-style execution.'

'But ...' Pratap said. The cockiness in his voice had disappeared. 'There is also the question of the alcohol which the victim had consumed.'

Ajay could see that Pratap was clueless now. He suppressed a smile and went on to hammer the last nail in the coffin of Pratap's theory. Ajay explained that at a blood alcohol content (BAC) level of 0.03 per cent, a person is deemed legally unfit to drive. At 0.15 per cent, the individual will not be able to walk in a straight line. And a BAC level around 0.35 per cent, which Chandrashekhar's blood report seemed to suggest, was close to surgically administered anaesthesia. So the victim could have hardly even stood straight. Suicide by hanging was out of the question.

'And then ...' Kumar began and Ajay nodded.

'And then there's the CCTV footage,' he said.

'What CCTV footage?' Pratap snapped sourly.

'We got CCTV footage of all the shops in the lane where Chandrashekhar's house is located. Several of them have captured a group of seven to eight women in burqas going up and down the lane, with the timing of their entry and exit corresponding with his rough time of death.'

There was a short silence. Pratap was fuming internally because he had ordered his team to check the footage and Ajay had clearly beaten them to it. Ajay seemed to read his mind.

'I'm sure your team would have got the footage soon, sir. It's just that I was working with a different theory and hence went after the footage first.'

It was an olive branch and Pratap decided to take it. 'Six to seven women, you said?'

Ajay nodded.

'The problem is that the lack of light and hence the grainy footage makes it impossible to discern the exact number. Which means that one of them could have easily slipped inside Chandrashekhar's house, killed him and emerged as a completely different person without the burqa, with no one the wiser.'

A silence engulfed the room before Kumar tapped his knuckles on the table.

'Thank you, Ajay,' the CP said. 'Both of you are capable officers. We can build from here and lead this case to its logical conclusion.'

Pratap was staring at the floor. Ajay shook the CP's hand. He hadn't revealed the serial killer theory to Pratap yet because he wanted to keep that line of investigation a secret until he found something more concrete. Already, Pratap's cheeks had flared and he was fuming under his breath. Ajay walked out of the cabin, sure that Kumar would subject Pratap to a verbal lashing at any moment.

Then Ajay glanced at his wristwatch. Damn, he was already running late for his meeting with Asiya.

9

Ajay drove towards Bandra as fast as he could. The traffic signal at Mahim turned red just as he was about to cross it and he stomped his boot hard on the brake. The vehicle screeched to a halt. He was the kind of officer who *usually* abided by the rules. He'd exercised great discretion when subverting the law even in his pursuit of terrorists and criminals. But this was a different game and he was already walking a very thin line with Asiya. He didn't want to give her a reason to walk away from him. He turned on the siren of his car.

The traffic constable manning the beat on the junction immediately took note of the familiar sound. He went to the middle of the road and blocked the incoming traffic to make way for Ajay's official vehicle.

Ajay put his foot on the accelerator, quickly killing all feelings of guilt. He wanted to meet Asiya, yes. But the meeting was also linked to his investigation into a sleeper cell. If not for love, he smirked, a man on the right side of the law could surely break a traffic signal in the war against terror.

The air shifted when he turned onto Carter Road. His life was far from the carnival evenings of Bandra, which was called the 'Queen of the Suburbs' in Mumbai. This cosmopolitan area was home to a multitude of Bollywood stars, cricketers and politicians. A sense of freedom and the rich carefulness of life flowed in the air. The promenade was filled with people walking their Dalmatians and mastiffs. Families from all strata of society were enjoying the scenic beauty of the seafront. The play area was filled with children lining up for their turn at the seesaws and swings. The guitars and saxophones of a street band sounded from a nearby amphitheatre. A crowd of onlookers cheered the band. Ajay allowed himself a prudent smile. There was something beautiful and democratic about this city and the country. He was duty-bound to protect it.

The coffee shop was located at the turn of the road. He parked outside and rushed up the stairs. Asiya was sitting at a table in the corner under an umbrella-like shade. The breeze was making her hair fly as she looked into the distance where the waves from the Arabian Sea were lashing the rocks. Her chiffon dupatta swayed in the wind.

Ajay raised his hand to wave at her but she was so caught up in the moment that she failed to notice him altogether. It seemed like time had slowed. Finally, she broke the spell and turned, noticed him and waved back.

He strode towards her. She tried to contain an impish smile. It warmed his heart that she'd taken the effort to dress for the occasion. Outside the aura of his official cabin, Ajay realized that looking into her hazel-brown eyes needed tons of confidence. He was worried that his shy politeness would mar any chances of her taking a liking to him.

Asiya pointed to her elegant wristwatch.

'You're late,' she said.

'Sorry.' Ajay glanced at his watch and then rechecked the time on his cellphone. 'I walked into an important meeting and lost track of time.'

'A man with a watch knows what time it is,' Asiya said. 'A man with two watches is never sure. This is called Segal's Law.'

'Impressive,' Ajay said and tipped his head. 'I knew you were a lawyer, but Segal's Law is more of an irony than legality.'

'Well, a lawyer needs to know a variety of subjects, Mr Ajay, to argue with the might of the state. Your

Sanskrit shloka-quoting public prosecutor being a case in point.'

This was the first time he'd heard his name in her voice. And never had he liked the sound of his name more.

A waiter arrived with the menu and she grabbed one. The waiter pushed a menu into Ajay's hands too.

Ajay flipped through the pages. All the items seemed Greek and Latin to him. The Blue Lagoon sounded like a stretch of salt water. He had no clue how to pronounce Macchiato. He was fond of coffee, yes, but plain filter coffee, which found on the menu after much struggle. When Asiya ordered a cappuccino, he watched the pout of her lips and listened to the pronunciation so that he could order the beverage the next time they met. And then he realized he was getting his hopes too high. What if there was no next time?

When the coffee arrived, Asiya perfectly tore open the perforation of the sugar sachet using only her fingers. Ajay consciously stopped himself from using his teeth for the task. Asiya poured the sugar in her coffee. He looked at her high cheekbones and sipped from his cup. Wow, he thought. *This* was the best filter coffee in the world.

Asiya was doing her bit to keep the conversation flowing. He could only respond in monosyllables.

'Sorry for yesterday,' Asiya said. 'My emotions overpowered my discretion.'

'That's fine,' Ajay said. 'Being thick-skinned is a prerequisite to policing.'

'So you are? Thick-skinned?'

'I'd like to think so. I've shed my share of blood.' He folded his shirtsleeve till above his forearm to show a scar caused by a grazing bullet in the Northeast. The sutures had dissolved but the scar hadn't healed. There was also a scar on his thumb. 'And I've paid my pound of flesh.'

'Don't be so intense.' Asiya smiled. 'Love can heal you. You know, right?'

'It can?' Ajay scoffed. 'I've never experienced it.'

'Yes. A state of imbalance can be restored by applying remedies with the opposite qualities to the imbalance. This is called the Doctrine of Contraries.'

'Deep. So you are into Greek philosophy too?'

'Of course.' Asiya laughed and raised her hand to cover her mouth. 'Are all NIA officers so secretive and intense?'

'I think it becomes a part of our mental make-up. Our successes are like eel eggs in the ocean,' Ajay said. 'Eels deliver millions of eggs under the sea, but not a soul on land knows about it. And a crow delivers just one egg, but it will fly onto the highest branch of the tree and caw until the entire jungle knows about its deed. We are the eels that no one knows about.'

'Interesting,' Asiya said. 'Now please tell me. How can I get my three clients out on bail?'

Ajay paused thoughtfully. 'You managed to get bail for Nazneen. But she is still on the department's radar. The only way she can get a clean chit is if we know for sure that she isn't involved with any splinter group or sleeper cell of a terrorist organization.'

'And how will you know for sure?'

Ajay leaned back into the chair. 'If you find out and tell me, I will take your word for it.'

Asiya seemed to understand this exchange. 'So, because I am her lawyer, you want me to dig deeper?'

Ajay nodded.

'I'm not asking you to spy on your client for me, or to violate any kind of client–attorney privilege. Maybe Nazneen is completely innocent, as are your other clients. But in my experience, innocents who are caught on the wrong side of the law are in that position because of their association with the guilty. In all my years of service, I am yet to see a person who was innocent AND surrounded by innocents. That just doesn't happen.'

'So what are you proposing?' Asiya asked.

'If your clients are innocent, someone else around them is guilty. Help me get to the guilty ones and I'll see to it that your clients go back to their families.'

He didn't know what to expect now. Asiya could easily throw a fit, stomp out of the coffee shop and never call him again.

Asiya sipped the last drops of cappuccino. 'Deal,' she said resolutely. 'The bail hearing for my clients comes up next week.'

'The NIA will not oppose it,' Ajay said. 'I will hold up my end if you hold up yours.'

Asiya smiled and extended her hand. He reached out and shook it like a gentleman. But once her hand was in his, he found that letting go was a tad more difficult than he'd thought. Her touch seemed to heal his anxieties and his fears. He wanted to hold onto her forever. She seemed to realize his conundrum and the impish smile was back on her glossed lips. She made no effort to draw her hand back. Finally, he let go. Her fingers lingered over his, and then she called for the tab and paid her share. She called for a cab using an app. And the damn cab arrived rather too soon, he thought.

As she stood up to leave, Asiya leaned closer to Ajay. She closed her eyes for a moment and when she reopened them, there was a certain playfulness. 'Is that your deo?' she asked. 'Or are there a lot of pheromones floating around?'

She turned around and left before Ajay could muster a response. He was zapped. Had she made a pass at him? His eyes followed her until she got into the cab. And then she was gone. *Damn.* Ajay took another sip of the coffee and found that now that Asiya had left, it had turned into the most tasteless beverage in the world.

10

Quality intel was the precursor to preventing a terror attack. And to gather such intel, one had to meet their sources, identify patterns from the data and prepare a lot of reports for the chain of command.

Later that evening, Ajay parked his vehicle at a police barricade near the Gateway of India. He'd come to meet a trusted source from another agency, Moshe Frischman, an Israeli agent who worked for the Mossad. Ajay was sure that that was not his real name.

Ajay walked towards the monument. A group of foreigners was headed towards Cafe Leopold, which was popular among the tourists. This area was often the first choice for terrorists who wanted to target the city. In 2003, twin bombs planted in taxis around the

Gateway had killed fifty-four people and injured nearly 240.

The iconic Taj Mahal Palace hotel stood tall in the backdrop. In November 2008, the hotel and its guests were held hostage by rampaging terrorists who were neutralized only after the National Security Guard and Marine Commandos stormed the premises. More than a decade had passed since the incident. Things had remained largely peaceful in the city since then, though the undercurrents were evident. Ajay could feel that the city was sitting on a pile of gunpowder. And somewhere in the dark alleys, someone was trying to light a match.

Moshe was hunching over the stone walls overlooking the seafront. He pulled out a steel flask from the pocket of his Bermuda shorts and gulped down a shot of whisky. His eyes flared with a tinge of red. Ajay stood next to him, staring at a naval ship anchored in the distance. The high tide lashed against the shore.

'How was your trip to Iraq?' Ajay asked.

'Terrible,' Moshe shook his head. 'The Daesh were all over the place, my man.'

Moshe described how the Mossad had planted him in the Saladin province, a stronghold of the Daesh – al-Dawla al-Islamiyya fil Iraq wa al-Sham – a group better known to the world as ISIS. While uncovering the sources through which money was being laundered into its coffers, Moshe had landed up at an auction – the barbarians were selling off young women to fight their dirty war. Ajay shook his head.

Years ago, when he was a young DCP posted with the Maharashtra ATS, Ajay had to learn Urdu and Arabic till he could speak both languages fluently. His next task had been to read the Quran and the Hadith in original Arabic, over and over, till any reference to any verse immediately made sense to him. It had taken him six long years, during which he was promoted to the rank of DIG and granted a deputation with the NIA, before he could claim some mastery over the religious texts.

'It's just the way things are,' his instructor had told him. 'The majority of terrorist organizations follow Islam and speak Arabic and Urdu, and hence, we must be well versed with their motivations – or supposed motivations. Had their religion and language been different, your study material too would have been different.'

This, however, was certainly not the religion he had read about in the Holy Book. He had read in the Hadith that the heavens were underneath the feet of one's mother. The Daesh were demeaning an entire religion and its people.

'Then,' Moshe said, 'I marched with a group of pilgrims from Najaf to Karbala.'

This 90-kilometre-long march culminated at the shrine of Imam Hussain, the grandson of Prophet Mohammed. The pilgrims carried black flags to mourn Hussain's martyrdom. In 2014, the Daesh had fired a rocket even at these innocent pilgrims. 'The Daesh see this as a stream of revenue, my man,' Moshe said. 'The government of Iraq pays a lot of money to the terrorists for letting this event pass peacefully.'

'This is transient peace,' Ajay said. 'It won't last.'

Moshe agreed. He went on to describe what he'd learnt from his source, a man named Abu Refai who had been part of the Iraqi secret service during Saddam Hussein's regime. The Daesh had made over 500 million dollars from the sale of Iraqi oil in the black market. 'That is ridiculous money,' Moshe said.

'How many fighters does the Daesh have on the ground?' Ajay asked.

'Twenty thousand.' Moshe shrugged his shoulders. 'Maybe thirty.'

'Overthrowing Saddam's regime stirred a hornet's nest, didn't it?'

Moshe agreed. Three top commanders of the Daesh were erstwhile officers of the Iraqi armed forces.

The roots of the conflict were laid by the American invasion of Iraq in 2003, which caused the power to shift to the Shia politicians. Two invasions and three decades later, there was no end in sight to this war. The sacred shrine of Askariyain in Samarra had been bombed by terrorists a few years back. Areas near the Samarra and Balad shrines, which had a sizable Shia population, had to be vacated. Where was the conflict headed? Ajay knew that India would not remain unaffected by the seismic activity emanating from the epicentre of terror.

'How does all of this affect the subcontinent in general, and India in particular?'

'The radicalization happens in various ways,' Moshe said. 'There was this baffling case of a young girl from India who wanted to join the Daesh despite the risk of being turned into a sex slave for these maniacs. If they are not stopped, they will shake the foundations on which the world exists. Truth be told, many Muslim countries are also fighting this monster.'

Moshe's assessment was in line with Ajay's information. India's Muslim population was second only to Indonesia. The country could have been a hotbed for ISIS activity. But so far, only twenty-one cases had been detected where youth had either joined or attempted to join the Daesh. Four of these known cases were from Mumbai, one from Kashmir, one from Uttar Pradesh and seventeen from the south, especially Kerala. ISIS had cleverly played up these youth with doomsday prophecies, references to a glorious past and a call to seek revenge for historical wrongs. Such a playbook was often utilized by extremist organizations across the spectrum.

Ajay realized that an ideology which keeps dragging someone to the past was completely incapable of leading its people into the future. Asia was home to three nuclear powers. If the flames of extremism were to spread, the entire region would be engulfed in a fire which could reduce the subcontinent to ashes.

'But you came here looking for something more, yes?' Moshe asked.

Ajay nodded. 'We suspect a splinter group of this terror umbrella has set up a cell in Mumbai,' he said. 'I'm trying to find out what or who their target is.'

Moshe scratched his chin.

Ajay was convinced that the agent had more up his sleeve. 'Have you heard something?'

'I might have,' Moshe said.

'Come on!' Ajay replied. 'How long have we known each other?'

'The duration of our association alone does not help me, my man,' Moshe said. 'There has to be an equal give and take.'

'Fine,' Ajay said. 'What do you want?'

'A friend wants to come to India. He needs a visa issued without any hassle.'

'Consider it done,' Ajay responded. He knew better than to ask who this 'friend' was. 'Now tell me.'

'A flying bird from Tel Aviv told me that you should be on the lookout for a group of women who are bent on creating anarchy in India.'

'Women?'

'Yes. Several women have joined ISIS. Female militants played a key role in the Easter bombings in Sri Lanka. So they are closer to home than you'd want. For all you know, they are already hiding in the underbelly of this city.'

The information was in line with Kumar's assessment of the situation. Ajay had a hunch that Nazneen was definitely involved with this sleeper cell. He thanked Moshe for the lead.

Walking away, Ajay glanced at the majestic dome of the Taj hotel, which had caught fire during the 26/11 attacks. The image of the burning dome had become a defining moment of the incident. Now, a flock of pigeons fluttered over it. Ajay thought of the many people who lived in this city, including the woman he was beginning to love. He wondered to what extent he would need to go to keep her and this city safe.

11

From his front-row seat, Commissioner Kumar enjoyed the rhythmic beat of music booming through the loudspeakers as two Bollywood stars danced to the beats along with a large troupe. This year's edition of Utsav, the annual cultural festival of the Mumbai Police, had top actors and actresses performing. The audience included civilians and police officers.

Asiya was seated a few rows behind Kumar. She had been invited as a member of the law fraternity.

The film industry never cribbed about performing for Utsav each year. Bollywood was already abuzz with plans for a biopic based on Kumar's stint with the ATS. The entire equation was based on trade, not unlike the shady world of espionage. When Bollywood's first couple had needed police protection following threat calls from the underworld, Kumar arranged Sten gun-toting personal security officers for them without any red tape. Months ago, a reigning actress was in extreme fear after receiving an extortion call, which was traced to Malaysia. The matter had been resolved only after Kumar's personal intervention. The film industry, in turn, obliged the police force by performing at their annual festival. It had turned out to be a good evening so far. But Kumar's jovial mood was about to turn sour.

Just as the performance on the stage came to an end and the audience broke into thunderous applause, Pratap came hurrying towards his boss. 'Sir,' he said. 'A suspicious bag has been found at the Central Mall. Bomb squad is on the way.'

Kumar immediately rose from his seat. 'Let's go.'

The show was allowed to continue as Kumar did not want to cause any panic. The message was relayed to the home minister's office. Pratap and Kumar dashed to the commissioner's official car, where the driver had already turned on the engine. Kumar rushed into the back seat while Pratap settled next to the driver. The siren was turned on and the commissioner's car sped towards the Central Mall.

At that moment, Ajay was driving through Mahalaxmi towards the Police Gymkhana. He was looking forward to attending the Utsav event, as it would provide him with some much-needed respite. He was also secretly hoping to meet Asiya, as he knew that prominent figures from the legal community were routinely invited. He found himself thinking about how she had such a grip over a wide variety of subjects, which made her all the more attractive to him, when his phone rang. Ajay touched a button on his Bluetooth earpiece.

'How's it going, my man?' Moshe said from the other end.

'It's going,' Ajay said. 'Your friend get in okay?'

It had been a week since his meeting with Moshe, during which time he had arranged for a visa to be granted to the 'friend'.

'Funny you should mention him,' Moshe said.

'I can't do your friend any more favours, Moshe,' Ajay replied.

'Ah, no, my man. It is my friend who is going to do you a favour.'

'O … okay …'

'Listen carefully. My friend tells me that a pretty dangerous man has been hired to eliminate your police chief.'

Ajay slammed the brakes.

'What the hell, Moshe?' he exclaimed.

'Just listen. Apparently, the plan is to lure the Mumbai commissioner to some mall with a bomb scare and kill him as soon as he shows up. The assassin is an expert sniper and if your commissioner gets within half a kilometre of him, let's just say the city will need to look for a new police chief.'

Ajay slammed his car into gear. He knew better than to doubt Moshe.

'Moshe, my man,' he said. 'I owe you not one, not two, but three.'

Ajay cut the call and speed-dialled the Mumbai control room.

'DIG Ajay, NIA. Any major calls tonight?'

'Suspicious bag ka call hai, sir,' the officer at the control room answered. 'Central Mall, Mumbai Central.'

'Fuck,' Ajay exclaimed. 'Fuck!'

His mind began churning. Truly, he had no time to lose. He tried calling both Kumar and Pratap, but telecom networks were already jammed as news about the bomb scare had begun to spread. Ajay was not very far from the signal where the ambush had been set up. But the traffic was constraining him. At this rate, he would only make it to the police commissioner's funeral. He honked, but the road ahead was congested. However, the other side of the street was empty. He had an idea.

Ajay moved to the rightmost lane. And at the first possible opportunity, he steered the vehicle over the divider and turned on his siren at full blast. The tyres rumbled as the car landed on the wrong side of the road. Now his training took over as he began driving the wrong way. At the academy, they had taught him high-speed driving. Soon, he was swerving left and right while keeping an eye out for the commissioner's vehicle, which could easily be identified from the insignia above its number plate. He was cutting close to the vehicles, dodging them at critical moments. Then he could see the traffic signal ahead and his eyes were all over the place, on the road, over the top of buildings. He heard the approaching siren of the commissioner's car and saw it at a distance. Ajay moved his car on course for a direct collision with the commissioner's.

From the terrace of a high-rise, where he had taken position an hour ago, the sniper also spotted Kumar's car and trapped the commissioner in the crosshairs of his rifle. He factored in the wind speed and decided to follow the target until the car slowed down at the signal. Then he would fire a bullet straight into the commissioner's head. And, with the second shot, he would take out Pratap.

Kumar's driver was aghast at the sight of the incoming vehicle. He tried changing lanes, but Ajay matched him move for move. The zigzag motion of the car threw off the sniper's aim. Before Kumar or Pratap could react, Ajay rammed his vehicle head-on to the commissioner's.

At that moment, the sniper fired. A bullet shot through the air. An empty cartridge clanked to the floor. The bullet broke through the glass and hit the driver on his arm. Kumar quickly exited from the other side with his pistol drawn. He took cover behind the car. Pratap and the injured driver also moved out of the vehicle and formed a protective cover around their boss. Soon, they were joined by Ajay, who had also drawn his weapon out. He placed a hand on Pratap's shoulder and Pratap nodded to convey that the commissioner was unhurt.

Pratap and Ajay approached the front and tail end of the car respectively, keeping their heads low. Ajay studied the angle of the bullet and had a good sense of the vantage point. His eyes fell on the terrace of the high-rise where the sniper was perched. Movement. He subtly pointed out the location to Pratap.

The sniper realized that his cover had been blown. He quickly dumped the weapon and activated his escape plan.

'There's the bastard,' Ajay said to Pratap. 'Go get him.'

Pratap dashed towards the building.

When Pratap reached the high-rise, he noticed a suspicious man in a black T-shirt and jeans hurriedly making his way towards the street. The suspect had a hood over his head and seemed to be avoiding eye contact. He was trying to hail a cab. Training told Pratap that this was his man, but experience also told him that appearances could be deceptive. He needed to be doubly sure. Pratap drew out his pistol and aimed it at the suspect.

'Hey,' he shouted. 'Stop!'

The hooded man immediately made a run for his life. Now, Pratap was sure. He thought of firing, but too many civilians were in the way. Chaos descended upon the place as people realized that a shootout was about to occur. Women and children began shouting. Pratap decided against endangering the lives of innocent citizens. He sprinted towards the suspect, jumped over the hood of a vehicle and began chasing on foot. The suspect made a quick turn and entered what eventually turned out to be a labyrinth of interconnected streets.

Pratap was close on the suspect's heels. A regular at many of Mumbai's marathons, he was up for the chase. He could hear the echo of his boots as the suspect moved swiftly from one street to another. For a moment, the hooded man disappeared from his sight. Pratap slowed to a stop and looked left and right. And then he saw the man climbing up a boundary wall.

Pratap managed to scale the wall in his first attempt. The suspect had inadvertently ventured into an empty, open space. Pratap now had a clear aim at the target. He fired a warning shot in the air with his 9mm Glock semi-automatic pistol.

'Stop !' Pratap said. 'Else I'll blow your brains out.'

The hooded man froze. With his back turned towards Pratap, he placed his hands on his knees and began panting for breath. Pratap could hear his laboured breathing in the air. But if he thought that the assassin had surrendered, he was completely mistaken. The suspect pulled out a Russian pistol which he had hidden in the front of his jeans. He turned around and took aim at Pratap.

But Pratap had seen this movement. And he was the first to press the trigger, firing three shots at the suspect. Each bullet pierced through the sniper's chest, one after the other. His blood began spreading over the black T-shirt. He thudded to the ground. Keeping his pistol aimed at the suspect, Pratap approached the fallen criminal. The man was dead. Pratap wiped the sweat off his face and called the control room so that the body could be sent for a postmortem.

'Sir …' the control room officer said. 'It might take some time, sir.'

'Why?' Pratap barked.

‘A bomb has been found at the Police Gymkhana, sir.’

‘WHAT THE FUCK!’ Pratap yelled.

Ajay looked at the blue bag from a distance.

He had received a call while he was shepherding Kumar into his vehicle. According to the control room officer, advocate Asiya Shaikh had spotted a blue bag under a seat and raised an alarm, after which one of the cops at the Gymkhana had informed the control room. The Bomb Detection and Disposal Squad was on its way, but Ajay got there first.

‘I can defuse it, sir,’ Ajay said to Kumar. ‘I have been trained in explosives and devices. If I have your permission …’

Kumar made a quick decision. ‘Granted.’

Ajay asked for a torchlight and a constable arranged one from the toolkit of one of the vehicles parked in the compound. And Ajay already had a Swiss knife, which doubled as a keychain. He would need the knife and the screwdriver from it.

Before he began making his way towards the bag, Ajay hugged Asiya and wondered if this was the last time. Asiya’s eyes were moist with emotion as she clung to him. He kissed her on the forehead. Halfheartedly, she moved out of his way.

Slowly, Ajay began to walk towards the bag. Sweat poured down his ribs. But he was in control of his breathing. He entered the row where the bomb was placed and bent to look at the bag.

He flashed the torch under the seat to ensure that the bag itself was not booby-trapped. Then he slowly pulled the bag and placed his ear on top of the zip. *Tick. Tick. Tick.* He gulped and examined the zipper with his fingers until he was sure that there was no trigger mechanism attached to it. Then he opened the bag.

The device was wrapped in a newspaper. He removed those layers slowly until he discovered a big box which was blinking with lights. He used his hands to signal to Kumar that he had found the bomb and it was active. But he didn't look at his colleagues or the woman he loved, who had now covered her mouth with her hand and was on the verge of tears.

Ajay checked the box's lid again to make sure that taking off the lid would not set off the device. Then he used the screwdriver from the Swiss knife to unscrew the lid. He gulped. Five wires of different colours were mangled together. He would have to cut three of them in the right sequence to defuse the bomb. Using the experience he had gained at the academy and in the field, he decoded the sequence. The first wire to be cut was definitely the green one. He cut it off in a jiffy. But even in his confidence, he was joyous that he hadn't been blown to shreds. The second wire to be cut was the red. This time, his fingers trembled as he slit the wire with his Swiss knife. Again, he was relieved to be breathing. He was a little unsure of the third and final wire to be cut. Which was it? Black? Or blue?

Sweat flowed off his forehead into his eyes. Under the pressure of the situation, Ajay was facing a hard time even telling black from blue. *Tick. Tick. Tick.* He used the torch to check the colour of the wires again. He cast one last look at Asiya and his eyes closed as he finally cut the blue wire. He expected an explosion but … the timer stopped.

Ajay raised his thumb in the air. A cheer ran through the auditorium. As he made his way back towards the exit, Asiya rushed towards him and hugged him again. He also wrapped his arms around her. She planted a peck on his lips and he kissed her back. In the backdrop of the thunderous applause from his colleagues, including the commissioner of police, Ajay suddenly knew that he wanted to spend the rest of his life with this woman.

12

In her safe house, Hafsa was pacing across the room. The TV was switched on. Although the K-e-M had planted only one bomb at the police fest, she believed its impact would be equivalent to the thirteen explosions of the Black Friday bombings in March 1993.

The 1993 bombings were deemed to be a response to the communal riots that had followed the demolition of the Babri mosque in Uttar Pradesh. Until then, it was unfathomable that an extremely large quantity of RDX – called kala sabun in local parlance – could be smuggled into the city, that devices could be assembled in factories and planted across sensitive points, timed to explode around a particular hour of the day. After 12 March 1993, Mumbai was repeatedly subjected to terror attacks, each of which would inevitably make it to the front page of every national newspaper.

Hafsa grinned. Her plan was to cause maximum damage to the police personnel. Yes, it was an act of war. She could imagine the headlines, the attention it would draw from the national and international media. She was basking in anticipation of her victory when the news anchor, who had been screaming about the bomb, stopped mid-sentence, listening to the feedback through her earpiece. A second later, Hafsa's jaw dropped.

'DIG Ajay of the National Investigation Agency has, just half an hour ago, defused the bomb that was planted at the Utsav venue …'

Hafsa's nostrils flared at the sight of the policeman she hated the most. A vein in her forehead throbbed. Her head pounded as if someone had hammered a nail into her skull. Unable to control her rage, she picked up a candlestand from the dressing table and threw it towards the TV, shattering it right in the centre. Her heavy breathing resounded in the room.

After her fury had found an outlet, she got to work. One by one, she started dialling numbers from memory, using a different SIM card each time. It was slow work, but patience was one of the many qualities that made Hafsa the seasoned operative that she was. By the end of ninety minutes, she had called up all her closest confidantes, instructing them to gather at the safe house right away.

By midnight, all the top-ranking operatives of the K-e-M were assembled in the basement of the boutique shop. Over a period of time, Hafsa had built a complex web of connections, all of whom had managed to camouflage their activities.

Hafsa stared at the grim faces around her. She switched on the projector and turned off the lights. A visual of a mushroom cloud rising in the air showed up on the screen.

'We must not lose sight of our goal,' Hafsa said. 'The destruction of this city is inevitable. We will destroy the enemy with their own weapons.'

Someone in the room asked a question: 'But how will we get our hands on a nuclear weapon?'

'This plan has been in motion for years,' Hafsa said. 'One of our most efficient operatives had trapped three Indian scientists and gleaned a lot of information from them. We will use this information to obtain the design of the prototype being developed under Operation Trishul. And based on this design, the weapon will be built across the border. Then it will be disassembled and smuggled into the hands of a guerrilla group who will fire the weapon into the heart of Mumbai.'

'But this is not going to be easy—'

'War is not easy,' Hafsa scorned. 'War demands blood. You think it was easy for the Iraqis when America invaded them for the second time?'

Hafsa picked up a pistol and held it in the air in a pose which was strikingly similar to the manner in which Saddam Hussein used to address his followers. She knew that like most dictators, Saddam's oratory had had great influence over his people.

'Our enemies want to battle against us?' Hafsa said with her gun still raised. 'Fine. We will give them the Umm al-Muharib!'

Hafsa had even picked this term from Saddam's dictionary. When Arabs want to signify something of great importance, they usually associate it with 'mother'. In the Arabic language, 'Umm' means mother and 'Muharib' roughly means a battle. So, Saddam had called the fight against the Americans the 'mother of all battles'.

'But there is one man, this Ajay, who is a thorn in our flesh,' Hafsa said. 'He needs to die. And I will put our deadliest operative to this task.'

Someone asked, 'Who is this operative?'

'The one who silenced the scientists,' Hafsa said. 'The one who can strangle a man with her bare hands. The one who leaves no shadows.'

'Where is this person?'

'Right here, among you,' Hafsa said, smiling for the first time. 'When the time is right, you will know who it is.'

13

Jonathan Hoffman had diligently staked out the upscale bar at the Four Seasons, Mumbai, before setting up the meeting with Moshe.

The training he had undergone almost two decades ago at 'The Farm', the top-secret training facility of the CIA at Camp Peary, Langley, Virginia, had now become second nature. He had identified the hours during which the bar would be least occupied and booked a table, under an alias, of course, for two, choosing one in a corner. The table's position was such that a pillar would block his face from most of the other patrons. A backdoor exit close by would provide him with a quick getaway in case the need arose. This was his third visit to India in seven months and he was taking due care to cover his tracks.

Thanks to years of operating in the field, Hoffman understood that the best disguises were simple. Real espionage did not translate into wearing stylish clothes and sleeping with beautiful women. In the world of spy craft, keeping your cover meant keeping your life. Hoffman had practised these principles and survived some of the biggest landmines in the world – Afghanistan and Iraq. In Southeast Asia, foreigners attracted attention by default, so he'd carefully chosen this upscale bar at Worli which was frequented by firangs. Now he was patiently sipping his drink while waiting for his source to arrive.

Hoffman and Moshe had collaborated earlier in Iraq, where they had conducted an operation together and built some trust on a personal level. This meeting, however, was going to be crucial. He was going to give Moshe a hint of the operation he was trying to conduct in India. And giving out this information meant playing your hand. But he realized he had to take his chances. Over the years, Moshe had cultivated many sources in the Indian defence and scientific establishments. Hoffman knew that such sources could, willingly or unwillingly, lead him to his objective sooner than expected.

His thoughts were interrupted at the sight of Moshe entering the restaurant. The Israeli too was an old hand at this trade. He'd taken care to wear a dinner jacket and formal pants.

The two men nodded at each other. Hoffman was all business as he handed over the menu to Moshe, who ordered a vodka without looking up at the waiter. The men spoke of mundane things as the waiter placed the drink on the table and withdrew from their surroundings. Then they got down to business.

'Our organizations have been traditional allies,' the CIA agent said. 'And so have you and I.'

'Of course,' Moshe said. 'We did good business in Iraq.'

'Well, I've got more business to conduct if you'd be willing. And this one means big bucks.'

Moshe held the glass in his hand. 'Talk to me.'

'The Indians are building a bird box, which will change the order of not only South Asia but the rest of the world.' Hoffman paused. 'It is in our best interest to not let that happen.'

Moshe was taken aback at the proposition, but did not let the surprise show on his face. In the world of espionage, nobody was a permanent friend or enemy. Such was also the case of operations conducted by foreign agencies in India. On 17 December 1995, a rogue Antonov AN-26 aircraft had airdropped rocket launchers, sniper rifles, pistols and AK-47 rifles in the village of Purulia in West Bengal. The pilot of the aircraft, Kim Davy, was supposedly a Danish citizen, but a credible theory doing the rounds at that time claimed that he was a CIA man who was then protected by the agency from being brought to justice. Operations like the Purulia Arms Drop, which might appear too far-fetched to the average civilian, were quite plausible in the playbooks of powerful spy agencies like the CIA.

Moshe weighed the offer Hoffman had placed on the table. The more he considered it, the more absurd it sounded. He ordered another round of his drink. 'The cowboys are okay with a *bird box* in Pakistan,' he said. 'But if India does the same, you always have a problem, yes?'

'We've witnessed the Great Indian Rope Trick twice,' Hoffman said. 'They are good at covering their tracks.' The Indian government had successfully managed to keep their nuclear programme under wraps during Operation Smiling Buddha in 1974 and Operation Shakti in 1998. After the Indian experiment in 1998, Pakistan had responded by conducting six nuclear tests of their own under the codename of Chagai-I and Chagai-II in the Ras Koh Hills of Chagai district in Balochistan. 'Having no clear leader in South Asia suits our objectives,' he continued. 'And yours.'

Moshe shook his head. He understood the message. But CIA experiments had their own costs. When the erstwhile Soviet Union had invaded Afghanistan in the late 1970s, it was an open secret that the CIA had helped the Afghan mujahideen with weapons, money and training. At the time, the Americans had no idea that they were creating the proverbial Frankenstein's monster in the form of Osama Bin Laden, who would eventually turn on them many years later. Moshe wondered if Hoffman was aware of the monster he was trying to bring to life with this new experiment.

'What are you trying to do, Johnny?' Moshe said. 'Let me guess. Save the world?'

'Oh, c'mon ...'

'Thanks for the drinks,' Moshe said. 'But I don't think I want more.'

'Listen, man—'

'No, thanks.'

'I understand you don't want in on this operation,' Hoffman continued. 'But I'd appreciate it if you keep my offer secret, especially from your Indian sources.'

Moshe stood up to leave. He pulled out his wallet to pay his share of the bill, but Hoffman insisted on settling the tab. Putting on his best poker face, Moshe nodded. The meeting had left him severely disturbed, and he decided to go back to his home in Colaba and continue drinking the night away. He was already in two minds about passing this information to Ajay or keeping his word to the American.

Ajay was preparing for another lonely night in his quarters. He'd sent his orderly on a week's vacation. The solitude, he believed, would help him cope with the pulls and pressures of the case. He was sitting on the couch in the living room, which had sunk to a point where he realized that the seats needed to be changed without any further delay. Requisitioning seats from the government meant going through red tape and he had borne enough of it for one lifetime. He was tired and dozing off while sitting with his head resting against the distempered walls. But the doorbell rang and shook him back to life.

He glanced at his watch. He hardly ever had visitors this late; it was close to midnight. He approached the door cautiously and looked through the peephole. Asiya was standing outside. Before she could turn and walk away, he opened the door and greeted her. She was wearing a pink salwar-kameez. Her legs were crossed and she was nervously holding the edge of her dupatta in one hand.

'Is everything okay?' Ajay asked, looking at his watch again.

She nodded.

'Come in, please,' he said.

He walked to the dining table and poured her a glass of water. When he turned around, Asiya was still standing at the door. He felt weakened by an emotion he had never experienced earlier. He stared at her for a moment, trying to make sense of the situation, and realized that she was in two minds about something.

Somewhere in the give and take of these things, she strode towards him with purpose. Instinctively, he placed the glass back on the table and gained only a moment before she grabbed him and kissed him on the mouth. His lips stiffened at first, but the brush of her tongue eased his mouth open. He finally let go and kissed her back with equal passion. All of this seemed like a dream. But he could see her and feel her and she was still there, holding his lips between hers.

An hour later, Asiya was in bed with Ajay, the bedsheets covering their naked bodies and her head resting on his shoulder. They were both enjoying the moment in silence when Ajay's cell phone rang. He grabbed the phone from the dressing table, trying hard to ignore her protests, and cast a look at the screen. Moshe was calling.

He dropped back onto the bed and answered the phone. Asiya leaned closer and placed her head on his chest. Moshe was drunk and he was pretty loud, such that Ajay was sure that Asiya could faintly hear him.

'What are you doing, my friend?' Moshe asked.

'Practising an ancient art at midnight.' Ajay chuckled. 'Remember that you are in the land of Kamasutra.'

Asiya playfully slapped Ajay on the arm. He grinned and put an arm around her.

'Fuck you, man,' Moshe said. 'I have no luck with Indian girls.'

'But you get lucky with information,' Ajay said. 'What do you have for me now?'

'Uncle Sam's nephews seem like they are up to some mischief.'

'Really?' Ajay said. He understood that Uncle Sam was a reference to America and the nephews were a reference to rogue CIA agents. 'Tell me more.'

'Not on the phone,' Moshe said. 'Meet me tomorrow evening. Same spot.'

'Okay,' Ajay said. 'Now let me get back to my art.'

Moshe laughed as Ajay cut the call and found the phone snatched away from his hands.

'I'll show you what art is,' Asiya whispered as she placed his phone on the dresser and raised herself up to straddle him.

14

Ajay was in that moment of his pre-dawn routine when he would abruptly wake up with sweat flowing freely down his neck. But this time, he could feel Asiya sleeping next to him, the warm touch of her body and the softness of her breath, and that comforted him in great measure. He realized, though, that a strong vibration was still pushing him towards consciousness. His eyes blinked open and witnessed a flashing of light in the otherwise dark room.

His phone was vibrating on the dressing table. The light from the phone illuminated Asiya's heavenly face. Ajay took a moment to watch her. He fumed at the idea of Moshe making another drunk call at such an hour and picked up the phone, only to see that it was Neeraj

Kumar calling. He struggled out of bed and went to the living room.

'Get ready in fifteen minutes,' Kumar said. 'A vehicle will pick you up.'

'Where are we going, sir?'

'We are taking a flight to New Delhi,' Kumar said. 'The home ministry has finally taken note of your theory regarding the deaths of the Indian scientists.'

'When will we return, sir?'

'Tomorrow morning.'

Kumar provided him a few logistical details before ending the call. Ajay realized that he would have to postpone his meeting with Moshe.

He turned to see Asiya standing in the bedroom doorway, smiling at him sleepily.

'I … I'm sorry, I have to …' he started apologetically but Asiya stepped forward and silenced him with a kiss.

'Do what you need to do,' she said softly.

Ajay looked into her eyes and saw no anger, no annoyance, nothing but support and understanding. He felt a tug in his heart.

He took a quick bath and readied himself while Asiya made coffee for both of them. The kick of caffeine invigorated Ajay and his pick-up vehicle arrived soon after. He kissed Asiya again and hoped that she would still be there when he returned.

An IAF chopper had been arranged for Kumar and Ajay at short notice. They fastened their seat belts while the pilots ran through their checklists with great alacrity. The aircraft blades began to whirl and Ajay experienced a moment of weightlessness as the chopper took off into the skies. Kumar briefed Ajay about what to expect in New Delhi. It was going to be an all-agency meeting. The Research and Analysis Wing (R&AW), the Intelligence Bureau, the National Investigation Agency and the Mumbai police had been ordered to attend this emergency meeting with the National Security Advisor.

They landed and breezed through security before hurrying into a waiting SUV with tinted windows. The glass looked like it was bulletproof and for good reason. The recent attempt on Kumar's life had made him a VVIP in terms of protection. No chances were being taken.

The meeting room was filled with uniformed personnel as well as black suits and red ties. Kumar and Ajay were seated not far from the NSA's chair who was going to take the first meeting. Ajay picked up a bottle of mineral water from the oval table and poured himself a glass. He noticed the sombre faces around him. There was a sense of common purpose, but the air was also filled with the chill of inter-service cold wars.

The Intelligence Bureau, represented by its chief, was India's premier internal intelligence agency. It had also been responsible for external intelligence between 1951 to 1968. Later, foreign intelligence was made the primary domain of the R&AW, which was formed in 1968 when erstwhile Prime Minister Indira Gandhi felt the need for creating a full-fledged service to gather external intelligence. The synergies between the two organisations were traditionally evident from the fact that the R&AW's foundations were laid by Rameshwar Nath Kao, who was then a deputy director with the IB. He went on to become the first R&AW chief. Kao's status in the world of spy craft was the stuff of legends and he shaped the R&AW into a professional and efficient organization in just three years of its establishment.

The National Investigation Agency or the NIA was formed in the aftermath of the 26/11 Mumbai terror attacks. The agency was empowered to probe terror attacks all over the country and held concurrent jurisdiction.

Nishikant Dobriyal, who was the current National Security Advisor, was an IPS officer who had served as director of the R&AW before picking up this sensitive post in the last leg of his stellar career. He was a polyglot who had a firm grip over many foreign languages. The kind of respect he commanded in the room could have only been earned by spending an entire lifetime in the security establishment and by putting himself out in the field and behind enemy lines. Like any other officer, Ajay had closely followed the NSA's career.

NSA Dobriyal began with a brief of how Ajay's theory – that the death of three Indian scientists was part of a series of planned executions – had gained weight after the R&AW had picked up similar intel from across the border. And this was also part of a larger design. A bigger game was being played, but Indian agencies hadn't been able to pick up its threads yet. More disturbing was the fact that only a mysterious silence had prevailed since the collection of this intel. Dobriyal now turned to R&AW Chief Rajendra Verma.

'Have the stations across the border reported anything suspicious beyond what we already know?'

'No sir,' Verma said. 'No chatter at all.'

'No chatter is not good,' Dobriyal mused. 'It means that the enemy has something to hide. Do we see any spike on NETRA?'

NETRA (Network Traffic Analysis) was a software network developed by the DRDO (Defence Research and Development Organisation) of India for the monitoring of internet traffic.

'Alert levels are in the green zone, sir.'

Dobriyal turned towards Intelligence Bureau Chief Priyanshu Dutta. 'Any LIM reports we should be worried about?'

The Lawful Intercept and Monitoring (LIM) was a project through which government agencies could conduct surveillance over voice records, SMSes, GPRS data, and CDRs (call detail records) of phones in India. It was through such surveillance that security agencies often kept track of terrorist activity. However, terrorists would also keep changing their strategies to stay out of the radar of the agencies. They often developed codewords, referring to explosives as 'mithai' and AK-47s as 'guitars', and so on.

The IB chief ruffled through the pages of a file he had carried. 'No, sir.'

The NSA now spoke directly to Kumar and Ajay. 'You are both in the thick of things,' he said. 'DIG Ajay has done a good job with the investigation so far. But we haven't been able to pinpoint who eliminated these scientists. All of them had a connection to Operation Trishul, so it is obvious that someone wants us to fail on that front. And then we had a bomb scare right in the heart of Mumbai.' He paused. 'New Delhi has reason to be worried.'

'Sir,' Kumar said. 'We are working on some crucial leads. We'll crack the case soon.'

Priyanshu Dutta fired a salvo at Kumar: 'Hopefully, you'll do so by catching someone alive, and not in an "encounter". We could have really used the intel from that sniper.'

Kumar was not in the mood to hold back either. 'Maybe if your agency had given us prior information that a sniper is going to land up in our city with an imported rifle, we would have been more alert.'

'Okay,' Dobriyal cut in. 'OKAAYY, okay! Calm down, everyone!'

He gave the room a minute to settle down.

'Let's touch base in forty-eight hours and see what we all can find. And, for the love of God, find something.'

After the NSA left, Ajay and Neeraj Kumar spent the rest of the day in more meetings with the R&AW and IB chiefs over the various facets of the case.

It was past midnight by the time they boarded the commercial flight back to Mumbai. Both men were unfastening their seatbelts upon landing when Ajay's phone rang. He smiled, thinking that Asiya was calling. But his expression changed when he noticed Pratap's name. He answered the call.

'I may have some bad news,' Pratap said. There was a sensitivity in his tone that Ajay had not detected earlier.

'How bad?' Ajay asked as fliers began collecting their luggage from the overhead racks.

'You tell me,' Pratap said. 'I'm at a rented apartment in Colaba, where one Moshe Frischman was found murdered this morning. And the last person he called was you.'

Ajay's blood ran cold.

15

A police jeep picked up Ajay from the airport. They sped off towards Colaba, where Moshe used to live in a nondescript house in the bylanes. It was a fair distance away from Chabad House, which served as the outreach centre for the Jews in Mumbai and had been one of the targets of the 26/11 attacks.

By the time Ajay arrived, Pratap had cordoned off the area. Barricades had been put up. There was considerable police presence on the streets. The constable parked the car near the bylane where Moshe lived and Ajay disembarked from the vehicle. He acknowledged the salutes from the other policemen as he walked towards the building.

A fleet of cars was parked on both sides of the road. Shop owners around the complex had downed their shutters for the day. Ajay could understand their predicament. '*Police ka lafda nahi chahiye* (we want no trouble with the cops)' was the most common refrain of civilians everywhere. Ajay climbed up the wooden stairs and squatted under the police tape to enter Moshe's house. One of the junior policemen brought over a pair of non-porous gloves and Ajay slipped them onto his hands.

Pratap was dictating his observations to a constable, who was making notes in a red diary. The living room was filled with cops. The body was not visible to Ajay yet. He found it ironic that people turned into *bodies* after their death. Their names were written in police records, but their identities were reduced to statistics and euphemisms.

'Where is *it*?' Ajay asked.

Pratap led him to a corridor that went to the other rooms. To kill an Israeli operative was not an easy task. A foreign-made pistol was lying a few feet away from his body, which was sprawled in the middle of the corridor.

Moshe's gold-plated spectacles were still on. The lens had cracked when he had fallen to the floor.

'Who reported it to the police?' Ajay asked.

'The Israeli Embassy asked us to check in on him,' Pratap said. 'His wife had called them up.'

'Where is his wife?'

'In Haifa,' Pratap said. 'She'd left for Israel only four days ago. The two were on a video call in the bedroom when Moshe told her that perhaps someone was at the door. He disconnected and never called back. He didn't answer her subsequent calls for hours either. Troubled by the sudden events, she alerted her embassy.'

'Did the murderer make a forced entry?'

'Yes,' Pratap said. 'She picked the door lock.'

'She?' Ajay said. 'Interesting.'

'There's CCTV footage captured by the store on the opposite side of the road. A woman with a limp made her way into the apartment around the time the murder happened.'

'Do you have an ID on the suspect?'

'No,' Pratap said. 'She was wearing a burqa.'

The gears suddenly started turning in Ajay's head. A group of women in burqas had been also spotted in the CCTV footage recovered from the site of Chandrashekhar's murder. Plus, there was the warning from Moshe himself about a module of women being active in Mumbai.

Still, Ajay was not the kind of officer who would solely rely on his instincts.

'Forensics picked up any fingerprints?' he asked.

'They've soaked the place with Ninhydrin,' Pratap said. 'But not one damn print could be obtained. The killer was wearing gloves.'

Ninhydrin was the chemical forensic teams used to detect fingerprints.

They reached Moshe's study. The killer hadn't left behind a lot of mess, but she hadn't bothered cleaning up either. Moshe's desk had been ransacked. Papers were strewn all over. But it wasn't clear if the killer had come looking for a document or if she had tried to stage the crime scene after the killing. On one of the walls, Moshe had put up the Star of David, symbolic of his Jewish identity.

There was a certain tension in the room. Ajay asked for the room to be cleared, except for Pratap. Then he took a moment to breathe and began to recreate the scene with inputs from Pratap. From the CCTV footage that the JCP showed him on his cellphone, Ajay could see that the killer had walked towards the apartment. She had climbed up the stairs. At that time, Moshe must have been engaged in the video call with his wife. Forensics had studied the dents and scuff marks around the main door's keyhole and confirmed that an improvised lockpick had been used. It could have taken the killer anywhere between ten to twenty seconds to break in. And, according to Pratap, Moshe did not hear the noise because he was wearing earphones during the video call. The earphones were still connected to his laptop, which was inside his bedroom.

Ajay put himself in Moshe's position. The killer would have slightly pushed the door open, making as little noise as possible. However, a trained spy like Moshe would have instantly detected the shift in the air – he was that good – and quickly told his wife that he was going to check on the door.

He would have been stealthy, trying to ensure that the intruder did not figure out his exact position in the three-bedroom house. He would have gone for his weapon – Ajay saw an open drawer in the study, which had probably housed his IWI Masada semi-automatic pistol, the one that was now lying on the floor. Then, a game of cat-and-mouse would have begun.

From here on, it was pure conjecture, but Ajay let his mind run with it. Moshe would have raised his gun to his shooting position. But he was already at a disadvantage. The killer had taken her position in the living room and aimed her own pistol towards the corridor. As soon as Moshe stepped into the corridor, the killer would have sprung from beyond the wall and fired two bullets to his head.

Ajay's eyes circled around the room and came back to a stop near Moshe's body. Kneeling down, he gently turned his friend's head around till he saw the two entry wounds. They were bunched very close together, indicating that the killer had superb aim and very stable hands. She had fired the second bullet only to leave nothing to chance.

Moshe fell in the corridor. He hadn't been able to return the fire. The killer had walked up to him to make sure he had died. She had probably not established any contact with the dead body to avoid leaving any fingerprints. And then she had rummaged through his documents to look for something crucial. Or she wanted to throw the investigation towards a different track. Pratap had checked with the shopkeepers whether they heard any suspicious noises and no one had heard a sound. It meant that the killer had used a silencer on her pistol.

Ajay thought again about the killer's motive. If she had to procure a document, she could have chosen a time when the house was empty. But she had come when the agent was inside and it was nothing short of putting one's hand into a viper's pit, because Israeli agents are amongst the deadliest in the world. However, the killer had completed her job with efficiency and walked out of the situation alive. There were no signs to show that she had met with any harm.

Ajay murmured a prayer under his breath for his fallen friend. He was just finishing it when a memory came rushing back to him.

'My man,' Moshe had once told Ajay, 'the secrets I carry will go with me to my grave.'

'And you're randomly telling me this because?' Ajay had asked, nonplussed.

'Let's call it a test,' Moshe had said, smiling enigmatically. 'Let's see if you're able to decode this puzzle.'

Ajay stood motionless and thought hard.

'With me to my grave …'

Ajay turned to the forensics team.

'Are you guys done?' he asked. The head of the team nodded.

'Turn the body over, please,' Ajay said and the team obeyed.

Ajay started searching Moshe's body carefully. He checked under the shirt collar, then under both shirt sleeves and both legs of his pants, but found nothing.

'I need everyone except Pratap sir out of here, please,' he said and everyone complied instantly, filing out of the house. Ajay waited for a minute to ensure they were alone before proceeding to undress Moshe completely. The man was very fair, like most Israelis, and his body was largely hairless.

Ajay went over every inch of his body before turning Moshe over onto his stomach again.

And then he saw it.

Tattooed at the base of his spine were two words in very small font. Ajay took a picture with his phone from as close as he could. Then, he enlarged the image with Pratap looking over his shoulder.

'What is it?' Pratap asked.

'Shem-kha,' Ajay replied. 'It's Hebrew for "your name".'

'And what the hell does that mean?'

'Let's find out,' Ajay said as he stood up and walked over to Moshe's laptop. He hit the spacebar and a prompt asked him for the password.

'Moshe once told me that he would take his secrets to the grave. Jewish last rites are similar to Islamic ones, where the dead are buried, only in coffins.'

'You're telling me that Moshe had his laptop's password tattooed on his back?' Pratap said incredulously.

'In a way, yes,' Ajay said as he confidently hit the keys on the keyboard and then hit enter. Pratap watched in wonder as the screen came alive.

'What did you type?' he asked.

'The Hebrew word for "invincible", which is the meaning of my name, in English alphabet,' Ajay replied.

'You know Arabic, Urdu AND Hebrew?' Pratap asked, impressed.

'Among other languages.' Ajay chuckled.

'No, wait,' Pratap said. 'Of all the people, Moshe tattoos your name on his back?'

Ajay's face hardened.

'It's a recent one,' he said. 'He trusted me. I plan to honour that.'

Even as he was talking, both Ajay and Pratap saw that Moshe's desktop contained only a single word file. Ajay opened it and a single page opened.

'Okay, smart guy,' Pratap said, reading the only three words on the screen. 'What in the blue hell is "Operation Dark Ages"?'

'I have absolutely no idea,' Ajay replied.

16

Ajay was facing an emergency at home. As a seasoned police officer, having held multiple postings at state as well as central government levels, he could tackle any investigation or operation. What he absolutely could not triumph over, try as he might, was his brown leather wallet. He was in the habit of tossing it into whichever open drawer he saw as soon as he came home and hence, every morning, he would have to go looking for it all over his quarters. Every day, he told himself he would decide on a fixed spot to keep it and every night, he would tell himself that he was too tired and would do it tomorrow.

Growing up in a lower-middle-class household, Ajay was habituated to saving his money to the point of self-deprivation. So far, he had resisted the lure of bribery. His mother had taught him about the sins of graft and the virtues of earning a livelihood free from malice, that did not endanger the lives of others. Ajay had understood this perfectly and his job paid him well enough to sustain his grounded lifestyle.

But he never skimped when it came to helping others, like paying for an aged relative's crucial surgery or sponsoring the school fees for the young boy who polished shoes outside the NIA office in Delhi. However, it was a different story when it came to his personal needs. Last month, he'd visited the Heera Panna market near Haji Ali to shop for a new watch and the salesman had shown him a piece which he had instantly liked. The price was just a little beyond his budget, but Ajay had restrained himself and settled for something cheaper. Which was why not being able to find his wallet always gave him a tinge of anxiety.

Now, Ajay checked the time on his new watch. He was getting late for a meeting with Kumar and Ranawat. But how could he step out without his wallet? A wallet with a wad of notes in its compartments was essential for a man's confidence. Ajay still hadn't become comfortable with digital payments. He liked the feeling of hard cash against his fingers. Having grown up without privilege, the feeling of money in his hands gave him a sense of security.

By the time he had searched half the drawers in his house, including two in the kitchen – he had actually placed his wallet in those more than once – he was suddenly hit by a realization that brought a smile to his lips: he wasn't living alone anymore.

'Asiya!' he shouted. 'Where is my wallet?'

He could hear the clang of steel utensils from the kitchen, then the subtle thud of her naked feet approaching. His orderly was still on leave and he planned to enjoy the privacy while he could. Living in with a partner was not a luxury available to government servants staying in government quarters, unless they wanted to set tongues wagging across the department.

Asiya appeared in the doorway. She was holding a ladle in her hand and he noticed that the apron she'd tied around her torso was still spotless. He admired the efficiency with which she cooked.

Leaning against the doorframe, she put on an expression of playful sternness.

'What are you screaming for?' she said.

'I can't find my purse.'

'Call the CBI, no?' She laughed. 'File a police complaint.'

'C'mon,' he said. 'I'm getting late! The CP has scheduled an important meeting.'

Asiya stepped forward and slid her wardrobe, right next to his, open. She plucked out the wallet from underneath her dresses.

'Here', she said. 'I needed to pay for the groceries last night. So I borrowed the cash from your wallet but forgot to put it back in your drawer.'

'Pickpocketing is a serious crime.' Ajay grinned and leaned closer. 'You'll be arrested. Let me get the handcuffs!'

'Don't you forget, DIG Ajay,' she said. 'I am also a lawyer.' She pecked his lips and moved back swiftly. 'And wasn't someone getting late for a meeting with the CP?'

'Oh yes,' Ajay said. 'I'll chargesheet you tonight. But let me file an FIR now.'

He grabbed her by the arms and they kissed again, but he was aware that there was not much time. Soon he was halfway out of the door and she was halfway back into the kitchen. Both of them cast longing glances at each other. Asiya blew him a kiss and he resisted the urge pluck that kiss out of the air and smack it on his lips like a teenager. He had to get back to being a policeman now. But before that happened, he wanted to imagine living with her for the rest of his life, with two children, one of them was a girl who'd look just like her mother. And he would come back home to all of them in the evening.

Ajay was smiling from ear to ear as he turned the ignition of his car.

Sitting in CP Kumar's office, Ajay tried not to fidget. He was updating Kumar and JCP Pratap on the progress on Moshe's case. Word from New Delhi was that the Israel Embassy had raised diplomatic hell. Moshe had been operating under unofficial cover and though they couldn't describe him as an official actor of the state, it was clear that his death had ruffled feathers.

'The job was highly professional,' Pratap said. 'Clean. Such efficiency can only come from an assassin of repute. This wasn't a mafia job with trails of blood all over the place. It was a cold and calculated hit.' Pratap recollected how Kumar had been attacked by a sniper recently, and the hitman seems to have entered India without even a blip on the radar of the Indian agencies. 'Perhaps there were two who entered the country at the same time and one of them got Moshe now.'

Ajay wasn't convinced. 'The suspect in Moshe's murder was in a burqa, yet knew exactly where they were going. I didn't see any hesitation in their gait. I'd suspect it was someone who had more local knowledge.'

Kumar had his own theory too. 'Perhaps the Iranians got him. They are forever fighting the Mossad.'

Ajay had to agree that it was a possibility. If this was true, it wouldn't be the first time that the Iranians and the Israelis had washed their dirty linen on Indian streets.

In 2012, a motorcycle-borne assassin had trailed the car of an Israeli diplomat who was working with the embassy in Delhi. When the car stopped at a signal near Aurangzeb Road, the biker attached a sticky bomb to it and fled the scene. The magnetic device soon exploded. The diplomat sustained shrapnel injuries but survived the attack.

Around the same time, another bomb was discovered under a car belonging to the Israeli embassy in Georgia. However, the bomb was defused by the Georgian authorities. Perhaps Moshe's assassination was another such relay between the two warring factions.

Just then, another thought struck Ajay, something that had been at the back of his mind all day.

'Sir,' Ajay said. 'The person we are after may not be an assassin for hire or a trained agent from Iran.' He paused, and it felt like the longest pause he would ever take in his life as the gears in his head churned furiously.

'In fact, I now have a fairly good idea about the killer's identity. But I will have to verify my theory.'

'You know something we don't, Ajay?' Pratap asked.

'I don't know it yet,' Ajay replied. 'But I'm meeting a gait analysis expert this evening, and I just thought of something else I need to ask him. Depending on his answer, sir,' Ajay said, addressing the last bit to both Kumar and Pratap, 'I shall have an update for you by this time tomorrow.'

Kumar was staring hard at him.

'Ajay,' he finally said. 'I understand you're a spy, and I understand that compartmentalizing information is like second nature to you. But if there is something happening in my city that I need to know about, then I want to know it before anyone else does. I am very serious about this.'

'Sir, if this is what I think it is, you will be the first to know,' Ajay assured him.

17

If Ajay could kick himself, he would.

The thought had started forming in his head even as he was talking to Kumar and Pratap, but it still took time to form. When it did, it took all his strength and restraint to not jump out of his chair and scream.

The discussion about Moshe's murder had got him thinking about the suspect in the burqa, and that led his subconscious train of thought to the burqa-clad women seen in the CCTV footage outside Dr Chandrashekhar's house. At that very moment, his cell phone had buzzed with a text message. It was from Asiya. It simply said, 'Miss you 😮' But it immediately formed her image in his mind and took him back to the first time he had seen her. That memory had dredged up another name in his head and caused the final piece of the puzzle to click in place. *Nazneen.*

Sometimes he wished he was more unrestrained, the kind of person who would express anything that came into his head and would be adored as the eccentric one. Maybe, he thought, his aversion to drawing attention to himself was what made him such a good spy.

The same tendency helped him melt into the crowd right now as he followed his target.

Nazneen walked down a crowded lane in Kurla, with Ajay discreetly following her in a Pathani suit, his face artificially tanned and kohl lining his eyes. A skullcap completed his disguise.

Ajay's suspicion was based on the axiom that the simplest solution is usually the right one. He had racked his brains looking for some mysterious squad of deadly assassins that had slipped into India in the dead of the night. What he had overlooked was the fact that you no longer needed to spend time in Pakistani training camps, thanks to the internet. Chandrashekhar's murder was by no means a job involving precise, surgical martial arts. He had been overpowered, injected with alcohol and hanged. Anyone with reasonable strength could have done it, especially with Chandrashekhar drunk and unable to fight back.

Same with Moshe. If Moshe had let his guard down and the killer had him at a disadvantage, it was just the matter of who pressed the trigger first. And, before he had arrested Nazneen, Ajay had had absolutely no idea about her background, physical fitness or abilities. As soon as they received the information about her being in touch with Pakistani numbers, the NIA had elected to move fast with the arrest. Ajay had wanted to spend some more time on surveillance, but the decision was a political one, and hence not his to make.

As Nazneen entered a tailor's shop named Perfect Cut Boutique toward the end of the lane, Ajay found a seekh-kebab–paratha stall and sat on a stool. He signalled for one plate.

Around him, three of his best men, also in disguise, were slowly taking up positions. One of them sat at a bus stop. The second entered a saloon and asked for a head massage. The third made himself comfortable on a concrete ledge at the edge of the road and lit a cigarette.

The stall boy handed Ajay a steel plate with four seekh kebabs, two thin wheat parathas, green chutney and sliced onions. Ajay placed it on his lap, keeping his eyes firmly on the boutique. As he dug in, he stole a glance at his watch. Around five minutes had passed since Nazneen went in.

Five minutes turned to ten and ten to fifteen before Ajay decided that it was time to move. He had finished his food. His colleague at the bus stop was getting increasingly uncomfortable with a young couple cosying up next to him. The one in the saloon had got his head massage and was running out of small talk. The one on the ledge had already smoked two cigarettes.

Ajay paid the stall owner and started walking. His colleagues got moving as well. At that instant, a swarm of seven to eight burqa-clad woman came out of the boutique, walking fast. Ajay and his team stopped in their tracks. They exchanged bewildered glances as the women fanned out, already losing themselves in the crowd.

Ajay swore. He pulled out his cell phone and called his office.

'Put out an alert for Nazneen Dharker. Arrest her the moment she is seen. Get Mumbai police to help.'

He shoved the phone back in his pocket and had just turned to run into Perfect Cut when an explosion threw him off his feet.

18

Ajay sped down the Mumbai–Pune expressway in his official car. He was on his way to meet Dr Mahesh Prasad, the deputy director of the Central Forensic Science Laboratory (CFSL) in Pune.

After the incident at the shop, Ajay and two of his team members who had been impacted were rushed to the Sion Hospital, along with several injured civilians. Since he wasn't injured too badly, he was discharged after a check-up and first aid.

It had taken all his strength and will power, however, to convince Asiya that he was fine. When he reached home, she had pointed angrily to the laceration on his forehead and then the cut on his forearm. He had to tell her the truth, after which she insisted he should rest until he got better. But time was running out.

Finally, after much pleading and convincing, she agreed to let him make the quick trip to Pune the same evening.

'You will keep your phone on the whole time and you will answer my call no matter where you are, or I swear to God ...' she had threatened.

Ajay reached the CFSL well before evening. The centre at Pune was one of seven forensic agencies across India, operating under the Ministry of Home Affairs.

Dr Prasad was waiting at the reception of the forensic podiatry division. This was a newly created division, which dealt with investigations around feet and the footwear at a scene of crime. Such investigation could then be used to construct a profile of the perpetrator.

'Thank you for meeting me at such short notice,' Ajay said.

'Of course,' Dr Prasad replied. 'Calls from the NIA mean serious business. What brings you here?'

'I wanted some footage analysed.'

'What kind of analysis do you need?'

'Gait analysis,' Ajay said. 'I was told that you are amongst the few experts in the country.'

'Well,' Dr Prasad said, 'I'll do my best not to disappoint you.'

The two men walked towards the lab. In the corridor, Dr Prasad explained that gait analysis was a critical component in the study of locomotion of humans and animals. A frame-by-frame examination of a person's walking pattern could reveal a 'gait signature'. This signature was generated by composite factors such as the person's posture, the length of his strides, the motion of his limbs, the tilt of his head and the angle of his feet. This signature was, arguably, as unique as a fingerprint. No two people walk in the same manner. The crime investigation department of a neighboring state had even used gait analysis to identify the culprit in the murder of a journalist who had a tendency to speak up against the current government.

The analysis lab was a complicated set-up of machines and wires. Dr Prasad switched on a computer, which came to life with a series of beeps. Ajay handed over an external memory disk containing the footage to be analysed.

'I have footage of a suspect captured from two different locations,' Ajay said. 'I presume that gait analysis can confirm, with some degree of confidence, if the suspect in both the videos is indeed the same person.'

'Absolutely correct,' Dr Prasad said.

Dr Prasad clicked on the first file. The two men waited until the file was fully uploaded to the gait analysis software.

The first footage was the one which had been captured from the CCTV in Colaba, in which a burqa-clad suspect was seen limping towards Moshe's house. Ajay was sure that the suspect had faked the limp to throw off the police, but he decided to wait for the specialist's opinion. On the monitor, the suspect was transformed into a three-dimensional model in hues of blue.

A link of blue and green dots appeared along the figure's axis, which was then plotted onto a graph. The results began to show up to the left of the window for each frame. The software measured the angle of the subject's trunk, hip, knee and ankle with each stride. It also measured the distance of the arms from the body in each swing. Dr Prasad made a note of the findings and then proceeded to build a gait signature.

'Do we know the gender of this suspect?' Ajay asked.

'Female,' Dr Prasad said. 'Aged about twenty-eight to thirty years.'

Ajay watched as the scientist opened the second video on the pen drive and uploaded it to the software.

'Give it a minute,' he said. 'The analysis takes time. I had them modify the software a bit to run all the same comparison twice, to eliminate any scope for error. Works wonders in court when we get on the stand and say that the tests were run twice. Solid piece of evidence for the prosecution.'

Ajay only nodded. The computer kept emitting ticks and beeps sporadically as the software did its work. Finally, it threw up a dialog box on the screen.

Dr Prasad thumped his palm on the wooden desk.

'Perfect match.'

Ajay took a deep breath.

'Dr Prasad,' he said. 'I need you to do me one last favour.'

As Ajay drove back to Mumbai, he stopped for a cup of tea near one of the many food plazas along the expressway.

He glanced at his watch. It was nearly midnight, but he decided to take a chance and call up a high-ranking officer named Nimit Shukla in the Mumbai branch of the Telecom Enforcement Resource and Monitoring (TERM) Cell. Shukla was one of several sources whom Ajay had cultivated over a decade of networking. Ajay had this uncanny ability to nurture relationships with people who could help him at the right moment. Undoubtedly, Shukla could dig out the information which Ajay needed so desperately.

'Where are you?' Ajay asked as soon as Shukla answered the call.

'Just about to leave office,' Shukla said.

'Real quick. I need you to pull me a favour,' Ajay said. 'Off the record.'

'What is it?'

'I've texted you a telephone number,' Ajay said. 'I need the location of this number on the date and time I am messaging you now.'

'What?!' Shukla almost screamed and then toned down to a whisper. 'That means I will have to log into the Central Monitoring System!'

'So?' Ajay asked. 'You have the access, don't you?'

'Yes,' Shukla stammered. 'But I also need orders from a superior. I can't randomly pull up numbers for surveillance.'

'No one needs to know, Shukla. I'm trusting you with a matter of national security.'

Shukla mumbled a few half-hearted protests about getting overlooked for promotion if he was caught in an audit of the system logs. But Ajay promised to speak to his boss, who was on good terms with the telecommunications secretary, and put in a word for Shukla's promotion during the next review cycle.

Ajay heard the click-clack of the keyboard as Shukla fed the information into the CMS, which was a clandestine mass-monitoring system by the Government of India. He could imagine Shukla seeing telecom towers blinking on a map and the view beginning to zoom in. Finally, Shukla obtained a location.

'Got it,' he said. 'I'm emailing you the number's movements for the entire day.'

'You're my hero, Shukla,' Ajay told him. 'Consider yourself promoted.'

Ajay got back into his vehicle and headed straight towards Neeraj Kumar's residence in Mumbai. He waited until Kumar stepped out for a morning walk, flanked by two of his security guards, before coming out of his car.

Kumar took one look at Ajay before hazarding a guess.

'That bad, huh?' he said.

19

A year ago, Nikhil Prasad, aka Nick, was a software engineer with the world's largest computer security firm, working out of the San Francisco Bay area. He had everything going for him – a large cabin, a seven-figure salary in dollars and a beautiful wife. He was well-respected in the community of technocrats and looked upon as a role model by the many Indian engineers who migrated to America each year.

But there were aspects about Nick's life which were not in the public domain. A few years ago, he used to moonlight as a black-hat hacker. He had met a group of Russian hackers and together, they had developed a computer virus that had caused widespread disruption in networks of banks across the world. But that was just one half of the story. No one knew about this, not even his wife. In office, he was the technical genius whom everyone admired. Using his position in the computer security firm, Nick had also developed a security patch for the same virus, which had raised his stock to an entirely different level and even got him an out-of-turn promotion.

However, Pakistan's ISI had not only managed to dox his identity, it lured him into a honeytrap with multiple women at the same time and recorded the act. They then threatened to reveal his hacking activities to the American authorities. It would mean a jail term in foreign lands, loss of face in the NRI community and a divorce from his wife. He had even applied for American citizenship, but if Uncle Sam would get the slightest idea of Nick's past, his American dream would come crashing down in seconds.

So the ISI had made Nick an offer. They would pay him more than what he'd make in ten years to build a virus that would disrupt the electron accelerator being developed by the Indian DRCI and the IARC. The device was named KALI (Kilo Ampere Linear Injector) and could be used as a beam weapon to target enemy missiles and aircrafts.

Nick was a high-profile capture for the ISI, unlike the pawns Indian agencies had intercepted recently. The last such instance was an employee of Hindustan Aeronautics Limited (HAL) in Nashik. He had been arrested for supplying sensitive information about India's fighter aircrafts to his handlers in the ISI. Such examples were not uncommon, especially in the age of social media. Social networks had made it easier for intelligence agencies to establish contacts with those it wanted to trap. Agencies would often set up fake female profiles (referred to as catfish accounts) and try to get in touch with government personnel who had access to confidential information.

But for Nick, the ISI had conducted a full-blown operation and successfully compromised his position. Not giving in would mean that he would have to let go of everything he had worked for over the last decade.

And so it was that Nick had flown down to India two days ago and was now sitting in a hotel room with Hafsa, his laptop up and running.

Nick stared at some coloured lines of code. 'I've been working on this project for the past three years,' he said with a heavy American accent. 'And I am close to a breakthrough.'

'Such attempts have been successful earlier?' Hafsa asked.

'Of course,' Nick said. 'There are many examples in recent history.'

In 2017, a cryptoworm named WannaCry had encrypted the data of more than 200,000 computers across 150 countries. To retrieve the data, the hackers had demanded ransom in the form of cryptocurrency. The total damage caused was estimated to be in billions of dollars.

'But Stuxnet is a better example of our strategy,' Nick said.

He went on to explain the evolution of Stuxnet, which was a cyberweapon developed jointly by the US and Israel to target Iran's nuclear weapons programme. The effects of the virus began surfacing in 2010. It had been introduced into the targeted network of Iran's nuclear sites through an infected USB drive. It had caused extensive damage to the Natanz Nuclear Facility.

'Such a cyberweapon is capable of complete chaos,' Nick said.

Stuxnet went crawling into the computer network over which Iran's nuclear programme was built and caused a series of accidents. In one instance, the operational capacity of the centrifuges at the site dropped by nearly 30 per cent. It also managed to shut down some centrifuges and caused a major incident at the site, due to which Gholam Reza Aghazadeh (then head of the Atomic Energy Organization of Iran) had to resign. The cyberweapon had damaged nearly ten thousand centrifuges at Natanz before the Iranian authorities could respond effectively.

'A similar attack will lead to the disruption of the KALI accelerator,' Nick said.

KALI was designed to work in such a way that if a missile was launched towards India, the particle accelerator would destroy it through highly focused energy beams. The project was such a secret that its existence had never been confirmed by India. If KALI was sabotaged, it would leave India vulnerable to attack. And that, combined with Ajay's death, would be the K-e-M's ultimate objective.

Hafsa grinned at Nick. He was working under duress, and it was clear that he had crossed a certain line with the country of his birth. She was aware that the ISI had trapped Nick by applying pressure at the right points.

But none of this made any iota of difference. For years, she had only dreamt of one thing. And she could now see her dream turning into reality.

20

Ajay was not a frequent visitor to luxury hotels. But the occasion demanded a certain level of style and hence, here he was inside the suite of the only seven-star hotel in suburban Mumbai.

Earlier that day, after meeting Kumar and briefing him about his findings, Ajay had booked the hotel room and called up Asiya, asking her to meet him in the hotel lobby.

Once she arrived, he had surprised her by taking her up to the room, saying it was theirs for the weekend. Asiya was delighted, but also a little reproachful about the expense. Ajay smiled at how well she knew him and waved away her admonitions.

'Asiya,' he had told her, 'there's a lot going on at work right now. The information I have on my laptop can set the entire country on edge if it comes out. The kind of people I'm chasing are evil to the core. Which is why I need some semblance of normalcy in my life right now. And you are the only one I can turn to.'

Now, she was standing in the balcony, watching a cargo ship approach the harbour. Ajay checked the fully stocked minibar. His fingers glided across the beverages – the Breezers, the bottles of red wine – and he finally picked two cans of cranberry juice and walked over to Asiya's side.

Ajay opened both cans, and handed over one to her. They clinked the cans as Ajay broke into a subtle smile while Asiya laughed wholeheartedly.

'Interesting,' she said.

'What?' Ajay asked, smiling, as they both settled into easy chairs.

'You never once asked me if I drink. And you've always offered me non-alcoholic stuff. Plus, I've never seen you drink either.'

Ajay chuckled.

'If you were a drinker, it would have come up by now. It didn't, and hence my most logical thought was to respect your choices.'

Asiya took a sip before she answered.

'I wish there were more in the government who had the same view about our community. Most government servants I have seen believe in mocking and insulting everything we believe in, just because we are the ones who believe in it.'

Ajay sighed sadly.

'I know,' he said. 'But my duty and my faith can coexist in harmony. And my allegiance is sworn to the idea of this country, to the Constitution of India.'

Asiya rolled her eyes, as if this was hard to believe. 'Speaking of co-existence,' she said. 'Have you heard of solipsism?'

'As a philosophical idea, it means that only my mental states are real and that I cannot be aware of anything beyond them.'

'So can you ever be aware of the existence of the *other*, the enemy whom you are fighting all the time?'

'I do not have the luxury of humouring grey areas,' Ajay said. 'Things are binary for me, most of the time. One or zero. Yes or no. Right or ...'

'... wrong?' Asiya said. 'Our moral compasses are guided by our circumstances. The person you brand as a terrorist may be a hero for somebody else, someone doing God's work.'

'No God wants the blood of innocents, of children, of women, to be spilled in their name.' Ajay paused reflectively. 'In the context of Islamic history, you must have heard of the Year of the Elephant.'

Asiya nodded, surprise evident on her face. Ajay was possibly the only non-Muslim who had even heard of this.

The year which Ajay was referring to roughly coincided with 570 CE when Abraha-al-Ashram, an Abyssinian ruler of Yemen, was marching towards the Holy Kaaba with the intention of reducing it to rubble. Accompanying him was a huge army of nearly forty thousand men, led by mammoth war elephants. Several Arab tribes who had tried to stop Abraha were swiftly defeated.

When Abraha was near the city of Mecca, different Arab tribes united to defend the Holy Kaaba. The Abyssinian ruler then sent an emissary to these Arab tribes saying that his intention was to only destroy the Kaaba, and if they let him have his way they could save their lives. Otherwise, they would meet the same fate as the others who had tried to stop his march. Abraha's army had also captured a few camels which belonged to Abd al-Muttalib, the grandfather of the last prophet of Islam.

al-Muttalib, who was among the defenders of the Kaaba, entered a negotiation with Abraha-al-Ashram. Surprisingly, he raised the matter of his missing camels.

Abraha was flummoxed. Here he was about to destroy the holy structure but those deemed to be its protectors were worried about a flock of camels. Abd al-Muttalib responded by saying that the camels were his property, thus he was bound to be concerned. The House of God, the Holy Kaaba, was in the protection of

God, who was its owner, its ultimate defender, and He would protect what was His and not let dishonour fall upon His slaves.

The next day, as Abraha was about to launch his campaign towards the final objective, a flock of birds (Ababil) appeared across the dark skies carrying small stones in their beaks. The birds dropped the stones on Abraha's army. And even small stones were capable of much devastation when thrown from great heights. The war elephants marching towards Mecca were reduced to pieces of straw. And thus the powerful Abraha-al-Ashram was defeated.

'God is the creator and protector of man. And this is basically what most faiths preach, when you get down to it,' Ajay said. 'Which boils down to the simple fact that there can be no justification for killing another innocent human in order to protect the God who created us.'

Ajay and Asiya continued speaking late into the night, and the more they talked, the more convinced Ajay was.

Finally, close to midnight, he stood up and went to the wardrobe. With a smile on his face, he opened a drawer and brought out the ring he had hidden inside. He walked back to the bed where Asiya was reclining.

She saw the case in his hand and shot up, now sitting upright with her eyes wide.

Ajay climbed onto the bed and slid close to her.

'Asiya,' he said simply. 'Will you marry me?'

Asiya grabbed his kurta lapels and pulled him close into a long kiss.

21

At 3 a.m., Asiya opened her eyes. She needed no alarm to wake up.

She turned slightly to check if Ajay was asleep. His back was turned towards her. She leaned over to his side and noted his closed eyes and the rise and fall of his chest.

After she had accepted his proposal – as simply as he had proposed, with a single 'yes' – they had made tender, sweet love and fallen into each other's arms, exhausted. Soon, both had drifted off to sleep, happy and content.

Asiya slipped out of bed and slowly, ever so slowly, picked up Ajay's laptop bag. Then she tiptoed out to the living room after taking one last look to make sure Ajay was still sleeping.

She placed the laptop on a table, but did not switch on the lights. The slightest noise could awaken Ajay and she didn't want to take any risks. She lifted the laptop lid. The screen came to life.

In the past week, she had obtained Ajay's login credentials through 'shoulder surfing'. Shoulder surfing was a social engineering technique by which hackers could obtain passwords of unsuspecting victims simply by looking over their shoulder as the victims accessed their devices. In the previous week, Ajay had had to log in to his work laptop from home for an emergency video call. Asiya had used that moment to slip behind Ajay and mentally note his password. By the time he turned around, she was already in the kitchen and he hadn't suspected a thing.

Now Asiya logged in and opened a chat website. Her contact at the other end was already using a virtual private network to protect his identity. Along with the VPN, he was also using various applications to mask his identity and make tracing difficult for authorities. His connection to Ajay's computer was routed through a chain of unsuspecting machines and networks.

With her contact online and waiting, Asiya started to search for the files that she wanted. The search took her deeper and deeper into the file directory. Some of the folders were encrypted and would have to be copied so that they could be decoded on another machine.

Sitting in the dark with only the light from the screen shimmering on her face, she was growing edgier by the minute. This was taking longer than expected.

Noiselessly, she typed out a message to her contact, telling him that she hadn't found anything and that she would try again later. She planned to repeat her attempt when Ajay was in the shower later that morning.

She quickly closed all windows, logged out and shut the laptop, plunging the room in darkness. Then she picked it up and stood up to go back into the bedroom.

'Don't bother,' Ajay's voice sounded in the darkness, making every muscle in her body stiffen. 'That was a replacement anyway.'

Ajay flicked on a switch and the room was flooded with light. He was standing in the doorway between the living room and the bedroom, wide awake, his face a mask of cold fury.

'You know,' Asiya said simply.

'I know,' he replied, equally to the point.

There was no point in lying, she realized.

With one strong movement of her arm, Asiya hurled the laptop at Ajay's head. He must have been expecting the attack, as he ducked almost as soon as the laptop left her hand. It sailed over his head as he rolled forward. At the same time, Asiya vaulted over the table that she had placed the laptop on. Both came to a stop face-to-face, inches away from each other.

Asiya attacked first, letting loose a volley of punches. Ajay matched her move for move, blocking or parrying each punch, refusing to give an inch of ground.

Within minutes, Asiya understood that it wasn't going to be of any use. She took two quick steps back and kicked out, her leg jack-knifing up towards his head. Ajay didn't miss a beat as he caught her foot in a vice-like grip.

Asiya quickly bent sideways from her waist so that by the time he jerked her foot to throw her off-balance, both her hands were already touching the floor. Using the floor as support, she lifted her other leg, swirled around in the air and drove the heel into his face, catching him squarely in the forehead.

Ajay crashed to the floor, letting go of her leg, and Asiya picked herself up. In the few seconds that it took him to regain his bearings and stand up, she had run over to the small table near the window, which had a fruit tray and a knife. She picked up the knife and pointed it at Ajay as he came rushing towards her. He saw it just in time and stopped a couple of feet away.

'Surrender now and make it easier for both of us,' he said.

'Never,' she spat, backing away towards the door.

He stepped forward but she was already at the door, unlatching it without even looking behind.

A janitor was clearing the dinner trays left outside the rooms. In a flash, Asiya moved behind him, grabbed him by the neck and put the knife to his throat.

Ajay stopped in his tracks. He somehow knew that Asiya would kill the janitor in a heartbeat.

'This isn't over,' he said.

'Of course it isn't, Ghazi,' she breathed.

The mention of that codename stunned Ajay for a second, and before he could react, Asiya was gone.

22

The suite had been completely taken over by the police. Uniformed cops bustled about. The laptop that Asiya had accessed was placed in a clear plastic bag.

Kumar was sitting next to Ajay, while Pratap was pacing about, supervising the collection of evidence.

Once Ajay was momentarily shocked into inaction, Asiya dragged the janitor to the staircase. There, she pushed him away and ran down the stairs, with Ajay in pursuit. She reached the lobby with Ajay still one staircase behind, cut through the sparse crowd and disappeared.

The police were now trying to track her movements through CCTV cameras outside and around the hotel, but Ajay didn't have much hope.

Pratap came up to him and Kumar.

'We're done with evidence collection, sir,' he told Kumar. In a minute, the senior cops were alone in the suite after asking everyone else to clear out.

'Okay,' Kumar said. 'Start at the beginning and tell me everything.'

Ajay started from the time he followed Nazneen to the Kurla boutique.

It had taken three hours for the fire brigade to put out the fire at the boutique. As soon as the site was declared safe, Ajay was the first to enter. He had already laid claim to the blast scene even as firefighting operations were underway.

Within the next one hour, the fire brigade and the Bomb Detection and Disposal Squad confirmed that no explosives had been used; it was a gas leak explosion. The fire brigade also opined that given the intensity of the blast, it was possible that someone had deliberately opened the valve of the gas cylinder, leading to a sudden rush of LPG in the air.

A body was also pulled out from under the destroyed shop. It should ideally have been charred, but the debris that came crashing down on it had saved it from the worst of the flames. Hence, Ajay could clearly make out the face through the partially burned burqa. It was Nazneen.

'With Nazneen gone, I had no way of proving that it was she who killed Moshe. The footage from

Chandrashekhar's lane was useless, as she was in a group. But in the one outside Moshe's house, she was alone. Probably because the murder was planned at short notice.'

'And so,' Kumar said, 'you went to Pune to get the gait analysis done?'

'Yes, sir,' Ajay replied.

Before Ajay left for Pune, he had collected the final piece of the puzzle. He had no footage to compare the gait against the one from outside Moshe's house. So he drove to the Esplanade court, where Nazneen had been produced for her bail hearing. He took a copy of her walking out of the gate with Asiya by her side. Then he left for Pune.

'Shit,' Pratap said sympathetically.

'Yeah,' Ajay replied curtly.

Dr Prasad inadvertently pulled the ground from underneath Ajay's feet, when he told him that the suspect's gait analysis was a perfect match ... but for Asiya, not Nazneen. Ajay was left shell-shocked and stunned. Asiya ...

Ajay desperately wanted to dismiss the theory, even as it began taking shape in his head. He was in love with Asiya and he hated himself for even suspecting her. But his job had taught him never to dismiss anything as coincidence without verifying every bit of information.

Asiya had been in his arms the night Moshe drunk-dialled him. The inebriated Moshe was loud enough for her to be able to hear him. And, one night later, he was killed. It was too much to ignore. Still, hoping against hope, he had passed on Asiya's number to his friend in the TERM Cell. The results had only confirmed his suspicions. Asiya's phone was switched off at the time of both the murders, and a criminal lawyer could not afford to keep her phone switched off for that long.

Ajay had driven non-stop to meet Kumar and tell him what he had found. Kumar had wanted to arrest Asiya immediately, but Ajay had managed to convince him to wait for twenty-four hours.

'Which brings us,' Kumar said, 'to your plan. Tell Pratap here, will you?'

Ajay nodded.

'After talking to Kumar sir, I booked this room and got her here. While talking, I casually let it slip that I was carrying some crucial information on my laptop. I had hoped that she would not be able to resist this, and I was right. She tried looking for the "information" on my laptop while she thought I was sleeping. What she didn't know was that I'd replaced my personal laptop with a replica, with certain modifications.'

'And I'm guessing that the fun part lies in these modifications?'

Ajay nodded.

'The best hacker on the NIA's payroll had programmed the laptop to spy on anyone who tries to break into it. As soon as Asiya started chatting with her contact, a hidden programme started tracing this person's IP address and relaying it to a team that had been on standby since last morning. Plus, the camera was programmed to turn itself on and record a continuous video of whoever was using it. If this case ever goes to court, that alone is going to be clinching evidence of Asiya spying on a government officer.'

'That's quite brilliant, actually,' Pratap said. 'So, who was her contact?'

'My team has already put him under surveillance. For now, I think we should just wait and watch. I don't think Asiya knows how much we know.'

'And what about Asiya herself, if that is even her real name?' Kumar asked.

'I think we should flash her photo across the country and issue a red notice in her name, sir,' Pratap said.

'I'm afraid I don't agree, sir,' Ajay responded.

'Why?' Pratap asked, a little irritated.

'Because,' Ajay said, 'that would mean revealing to the country not only what Asiya is wanted for, but the existence of the K-e-M. And the country would go batshit insane if that came out.'

There was a silence. Both Kumar and Pratap had to agree.

Finally, Kumar spoke.

'Anything else we should know, Ajay?' he asked.

Ajay paused for just a moment while his mind flashed back to the last thing Asiya had said to him.

'Of course it isn't, Ghazi.'

Aloud, he said, 'No, sir.'

23

Mahesh Dhoble was making his way into the Sheldonian Theatre of the Oxford University for the graduation ceremony of the academic year of 2023. He had arrived late and could see his son standing with the other students. His son was looking around worriedly for his father. Both caught each other's eye as Dhoble was taking his seat, and smiled at each other.

Dhoble had got late because he had romped all night with a young foreigner whom he had met at his hotel bar. He had taken her back to his room for a wild night filled with sex and drugs. Next morning, he had trouble waking up, but somehow made it to his son's graduation.

Dhoble's son climbed up the stairs of the stage to collect his graduation degree. The father clapped the loudest and resisted the urge to whistle aloud.

Dhoble was the chief of security at the Indian Atomic Research Centre. He had taken the last few weeks off to spend some time with his son. As he held a sensitive posting, it was not unusual for the government to attach a security detail for him. The security detail not just provided cover to high-ranking officers but also kept an eye on their conduct. This was to ensure that the officer would not expose himself, by choice or otherwise, to foreign intelligence agencies.

Intelligence agencies often tried to recruit high-ranking officers to their team on such visits. The most famous of such incidents was the case of Rabinder Singh, a R&AW officer who was trapped by the CIA at a foreign station and turned into a double agent. When he was detected by the R&AW's counterintelligence in 2004, Singh fled to the USA, where it is believed that he was killed in a road accident in 2016 after the CIA abandoned him.

But Dhoble had served the establishment for thirty-five years and was beyond suspicion. Therefore, he had had no security detail to hinder his escapades the previous night.

After his son collected the degree, he posed with Dhoble for a selfie when the father and son were photobombed by another gentleman in a three-piece suit. Dhoble's smile vanished when he saw the man in his photo.

'Young man,' Khush Dil said to Dhoble's son, even as he put his arm around Dhoble's shoulder, 'your father must be very proud today.'

'Thank you,' Dhoble's son said. 'I've met most of Daddy's friends, but I don't think I've met you before?'

Dhoble cleared his throat. 'He is—'

'I am a friend of your dad for special occasions, sonny boy,' Khush Dil interjected. 'Mahesh, why don't we talk in private?'

Dhoble patted his son's shoulder and asked him to carry on. His head suddenly felt heavy. He knew Khush Dil Khan, a freelance operative occasionally used by Indian intelligence agencies for dirty work. And the reason why he was used only occasionally was because KD, as he was known, had a nasty habit of popping up when you least expected him, to call in favours. These favours always cost someone or the other very dearly.

The two men began walking towards the lush gardens, crossing students who had degrees in their hands and the promise of a bright future on their faces. Dhoble's face, however, was drowning in worry. He had no clue what Khush Dil had up his sleeve at this time.

'Mahesh, allow me to tell you a story,' Khush Dil said.

What choice did Dhoble have except to listen?

Khush Dil continued without waiting for an answer: 'I once took on the job of stealing a classified document from a secure facility in Lebanon …'

He had first conducted a recce of the facility, noting the placement of the security guards and the cameras' blind spots. In the cover of the night, he'd managed to breach the facility and get his hands on the file. But just as he was about to exit the facility with the file hidden in his jacket, he was apprehended by the guards, who beat the living hell out of him and locked him in a cell.

'Now I was flat on the floor of my cell, every bone in my body broken,' Khush Dil said. 'I was to face a firing squad at the break of dawn, and I kept waiting for the sun to rise so that it would put me out of my misery.'

But a miracle happened: the cell door opened and the chief of security of that facility walked inside, holding a copy of the file which Khush Dil had attempted to steal. The chief handed over the copy to Khush Dil.

'You came here for this information?' he asked.

Khush Dil looked over the file. It contained the information he had come looking for. 'Yes.'

'It can be yours,' the chief said, 'for one million dollars.'

Khush Dil was stunned. He had risked life and limb when the file could have been obtained for less than half of what he was being paid for this job. He asked to make a phone call, which the chief allowed. A few hours later, the money was deposited in an account number provided by the chief, and Khush Dil had walked out of the cell with a fractured leg. But he was alive and he had the file; it was all that mattered. The chief got his money and the original file was still secure because he had provided Khush Dil with a copy, so nobody suspected him either.

'This mission happened early in my career,' Khush Dil said. 'And it taught me an important lesson. One should not risk one's life for a problem which money can solve.'

'Why are you telling me all this?' Dhoble asked.

'Because for five million dollars, you will provide me access to the IARC computer network. My job will only take a few minutes. No one will ever know.'

'Are you out of your fucking mind?!' Dhoble said, struggling to keep his voice down. 'I am not going to betray my country.'

'Easy, tiger.' Khush Dil leaned towards Dhoble's ear. He took out his phone and played a video file. 'You don't want your son to see this.'

The video was a recording from the previous night, of Dhoble screwing the young foreigner. Dhoble knew he was done for. Khush Dil had royally fucked him. There were close-up frames of Dhoble snorting lines of cocaine from the dressing table. It looked disgusting on camera – he with his fat and hairy stomach mounting the slim young girl. And then, there were the drugs and the alcohol. All of this would burn his reputation to the ground.

'I've had the good fortune of tracking your career, Mahesh,' said Khush Dil.

Dhoble's career was a distinguished one. Before being posted to the IARC, he had served with the Anti-Narcotics Cell and gained massive coverage in the media for wiping out drug cartels and the peddlers from the streets of Mumbai. Huge quantities of cocaine and heroin were seized under his supervision. From nightclubs and rave parties, Dhoble had confiscated sizable quantities of Mephedrone, also known as 4-methyl ephedrone in scientific parlance and Meow Meow among its consumers.

But no one had noticed that the seizures were being recorded in smaller quantities than the actual, or that drugs were being pilfered from the storerooms of the Anti-Narcotics Cell. Dhoble had discreetly distributed the drugs he had confiscated back in the market at higher prices and made a killing out of it.

'Imagine how the home minister will explain your benami land worth Rs 23 crore in Wardha,' Khush Dil said and pointed to the video. 'And how will you explain snorting that white powder?'

Dhoble's eyes widened. Khush Dil could sense his fear. He went for the kill.

'You were the darling of the media when you closed down illegal brothels on Grant Road in the late 1990s,' he continued. 'Imagine how excited they will be to play your sex tape with this young foreigner.' He paused. 'What will your wife think?'

Dhoble had a tough decision to make. He looked dazed and confused.

'Let me show the video to your son and his friends.' Khush Dil began moving towards the spot where Dhoble's son was talking to his batchmates with a big smile on his face. 'They can help you decide your future course of action.'

Dhoble grabbed Khush Dil by the arm. 'Okay … okay,' he pleaded in a broken voice. 'I'll do what you want.'

Khush Dil patted him on the back. 'Good choice, my man.' He turned around to leave. 'See you back in Mumbai.'

As KD walked away, leaving a devastated Dhoble in his wake, he sent a single word message to Hafsa.

'Mubarak.'

24

The gym's air-conditioner provided no respite. Asiya's heart was burning with the heat of a thousand suns. With each repetition of the deadlift, she felt the pain rip through her muscles. Her stoic reflection stared back from the mirror. But in her mind there was just one image, that of Ajay; and the smile she imagined on his face caused her chest to swell with deep, passionate hatred.

She took a deep breath as she lifted a 140-pound barbell from the floor and straightened her back. She locked her hips and knees as she held the weight. Beads of sweat dripped down her neck.

She dropped the weight with a massive sound of clanging of plates on each sight. For a slender woman like her, lifting four plates of forty-five pounds on each side was quite a challenge. Asiya's rage had made the weight seem much lighter.

However, this weight was nothing compared to the load she had carried since she was barely out of her teens, for the last twelve years.

She remembered the night clearly – the first time she saw Ajay from her hiding place in the Abbottabad mansion, amidst all the chaos and confusion. The first thing she'd noticed were his eyes, which burned with an unusual intensity. But what also caught her attention was the way in which Ajay held his gun.

Most soldiers or policemen held their pistol with one hand and supported it with the other, placing the palm of the supporting hand directly below the butt of their pistol. Ajay, however, held the wrist of his gun hand with his supporting hand. It was something that had stuck in her memory.

She had spent years trying to figure out the identity of the masked man with the peculiar way of holding his gun, but it was only after news of the encounter in Kashmir was published that she found him. Any good spy always reads the newspapers of the enemy nation, and Asiya would make it a point to peruse all the Indian newspapers that she could get her hands on. The Kashmir encounter had made the headlines in every major newspaper, and some of them carried pictures of the security team. Although the men wore masks to hide their identities, the leader was holding his pistol in the same way: with his left hand gripping his right wrist.

From then on, it was just the matter of tapping the right sleeper agents to ascertain his identity. The Indian intelligence community did not even have an inkling of how deeply the K-e-M had infiltrated their ranks. As soon as she found out his name, she went online and tracked him down on social media. His face made her heart skip a beat. She knew that face. She had seen this man before; he used to accompany the doctor on his visits to the mansion.

By this time, her plan in Mumbai was well underway. She already had a fully functioning cover as a lawyer, and fate dealt her a good hand when Ajay came to the city to investigate Chandrashekhar's death. The next step was to get close to Ajay by defending the accused arrested by the NIA.

The rest was easy. Asiya was as attractive with her face uncovered as she was lethal with her face hidden, and also fully aware of the effect she had on men. At the first sign of attraction from Ajay, she had shown ten-fold reciprocation and reeled him in.

During the inception of the K-e-M, the sisterhood had learned one very valuable lesson: being a woman was more of a strength than a weakness. Granted, nature had made them physically slightly weaker than men, but this was nothing that could not be taken care of with the right training. Recruits were taken to Pakistan via Dubai and then to a top-secret training camp in Afghanistan, where the fiercest of fighters imparted the most gruelling training to them. For three months, they were stripped of all their dignity and made to perform drills and exercises that made their very cores ache. Half of them ran away within the first month. But they had nowhere to go, being trapped in a foreign land with no documents. The only option was the illegal flesh trade, so most of them came back. Once they did, they were subjected to even more cruel training. Day after day, their bodies were toughened while their souls were drained of any humanity. At the end of their training period, brutal exercise and constant alertness became a way of life.

Then followed another three-month training period in another camp where they were taught to dismantle and assemble guns, make and defuse bombs and use daggers and other tools of close combat. All the while, they were given good food, expensive skincare and massages, so that their looks were not marred by their hard lives. They learned to take care of their God-given beauty.

The last month was a crash course in the art of seduction. When it came to women, according to their leader, men would always be dogs with their tongues hanging out. All they needed was a push in the right direction. They didn't need more than a month to understand how to do that.

The K-e-M had spent months planning the double attack – the hit on Kumar coupled with the bomb blast at Utsav. Asiya was always meant to 'find' the bomb exactly when the city's streets would be clogged with traffic following Kumar's death. A police commissioner getting shot would automatically mean most of the city's police force rushing to the crime scene. As a result, the Bomb Detection and Disposal Squad would never make it to the Utsav venue in time. The K-e-M had recently learned how to put together a time bomb with its timer *inside* the bomb, as opposed to face up, with the numbers counting down for everyone to see. This way, no one would know when the bomb was supposed to go off and even though civilians would have been cleared away, the bomb would have taken dozens of policemen with it. The police force had always been the target.

Only Ajay fucking Rajvardhan had first averted Kumar's death and then managed to get to Utsav in time to defuse the bomb. Thinking on her feet, Asiya knew what she had to do. As soon as he put the bomb out of action, she had rushed to Ajay and hugged him, and the way he hugged her back told her all she needed to know. For added effect, she planted a kiss on his lips and the bastard was hooked that very moment. Policeman or no policeman, few people could stay strong in the face of such intense display of affection immediately after a life-threatening situation. It was basic human psychology.

Asiya still had no idea what had given her away and how Ajay had gotten wise to her true intentions. But that didn't matter anymore. Their plans were already underway.

Now, as Asiya clanged the weights down on the mat for the final time, she allowed herself to smile. Ajay would die such a painful death that it would send a shiver down the spine of all humanity.

25

It was early in the morning but the IARC was already teeming with activity. Research was a continuous process and they couldn't afford any breaks. Work never stopped here, with people coming in shifts.

As a result, the security of the place, too, had to be monitored round the clock. Dhoble ran a tight ship. The former cop had always prided himself on his commitment to his work and was known to be a strict taskmaster. His subordinates lived in mortal fear of being caught napping on the job.

When he took up this assignment, Dhoble decided that he would do it with all his heart. He had already made enough 'extra income' in his previous job to ensure a quality education for his only son and a comfortable retired life, and this second innings paid much better anyway, which meant there was no reason to be corrupt.

That is until the cursed Khush Dil Khan came back into his life, Dhoble, now back in India, thought bitterly as he paced up and down the parking lot of his workplace.

He glanced at his watch for the hundredth time, absurdly hoping that time would pass slower if he kept tracking it. It didn't. At exactly 8 a.m., a car slowed to a stop and two men got out. One was Khush Dil and the other was a young man Dhoble had never seen before. Both were clad in crisp formals. Khush Dil's beard was neatly trimmed and shaped and the other man was cleanshaven. Their leather shoes shone in the morning sunlight. They walked to where Dhoble was standing, and without a word, he turned around and led them inside.

He signed in the two men as visitors, got them passes and ushered them through a door. They went to the central server room. There were five armed security guards standing at various points. The senior-most came forward, concern written all over his face.

'Everything okay, sir?' he asked.

'We'll find out, won't we?' Dhoble said sternly. 'I'm conducting a surprise security check. These are independent cyber experts who shall look for any breach in our system.'

The senior guard's concern doubled.

'There's been no lapse from our side, sir ...'

'You will kindly let me be the judge of that, Sakpal!' Dhoble growled. 'Now open the door.'

Sakpal complied immediately. He swiped his key card and the doors to the server room slid open. Dhoble and the two men stepped inside and the doors sucked shut.

'Nicely done!' Khush Dil exclaimed softly, patting Dhoble's shoulder. Dhoble shrugged off his hand angrily.

'Make it fast,' was all he said.

The other man, who was none other than the hacker Nick, was already unzipping his backpack and removing a laptop. He processed to fish out several cables and plugged them into his computer, inserting the other ends into various jacks in the central server. He then sat down on the floor and starting tapping away at the keyboard.

'Why, man,' Dhoble said softly to KD. 'Why this? Do you realize what it is we do over here?'

Khush Dil leaned against a wall.

'You know how I started in this line of work, I presume?'

Dhoble nodded. KD's father, Reham Dil Khan, had been one of don Karim Lala's closest associates, so close that he had been in the front of Lala's funeral procession when the gangster died.

In the late 1980s, a young Khush Dil was put on a flight to the UK to study at Oxford University. Every month, his father would send him money through hawala operators, which ultimately sent the young man spiralling into the world of crime.

Khush Dil was fascinated by how suitcases full of money could be moved across continents with codes written on the back of currency notes and telephone calls which lasted only a few seconds. Soon, he too entered the hawala business.

But one of the deals went wrong in 1991 and Khush Dil was deported to India, where he was charged under the prevailing foreign exchange management laws. While the trial was in progress, he was lodged at Arthur Road Jail. An ordinary youngster would have learned a lesson or two about the law by now, but Khush Dil had been brought up in a family that had always worn a jail sentence like a badge of honour. He had grown up listening to his father talk about how to survive in prison. So, the incarceration was much like a ritual to announce his arrival into the world of crime.

There was only one more high-profile prisoner in Arthur Road apart from KD at the time – a slightly built middle-aged man named Harshesh Mehra, who was imprisoned for a series of financial frauds that had left the stock market in ruins. Mehra had no backing or godfather, but he had a lot of money hidden away, which made him the prime target for many an old salt in the prison gang hierarchy.

KD immediately saw an opportunity. Using his connections to the Karim Lala gang as well as his considerable physical strength, he appointed himself as Mehra's personal bodyguard. He would walk alongside the nervous Mehra as the latter traversed the risk-ridden corridors of the human zoo and rebuff any predatory attempts with a well-aimed punch to the nose or gut.

Mehra took a liking to the brawny youngster and the duo began spending more time together. During a casual conversation, Mehra mentioned that he had Rs 2,000 crore of Indian currency stuck in the Cayman Islands. He wanted to move this money to Hong Kong first and then to various banks in India. Mehra's network was already under the scanner, so he was looking for a man who could pull off this job. Khush Dil volunteered for the task even as Mehra's jaw nearly hit the floor on seeing the young man's confidence.

'But,' Khush Dil said, 'I need my commission for the job.'

'How much?' Mehra asked.

'Ten per cent.'

For a man who was sitting on one of the tallest stacks of currency notes in the country, Mehra was a tough customer. 'Too much,' he replied. 'Five is fair.'

The two men shook hands. As a litmus test, Khush Dil was tasked to move the first tranche of Rs 50 crore. He began relaying information to his partners in the UK through the lawyers who would come to meet him at the jail, who were promised a good cut. Mehra was pleasantly shocked when his contacts confirmed that the first tranche had landed in their benami accounts, which had not been discovered by the cops.

And then, over a period of two months, KD moved the entire Rs 2,000 crore to India. Mehra stayed good on his promise and paid Rs 100 crore to KD. So, by the time KD stepped out of Arthur Road Jail after being acquitted of all charges for lack of evidence, he was already a rich man. The first thing he did was to purchase a sea-facing villa in Bandra and a Rolls-Royce.

'Money is power, Mahesh,' KD now said to Dhoble. 'Money and information. There is information in that server, and I'm getting money in exchange for it. That's all that matters. Everything else – your ideals, your emotions and whatnot – everything else is an illusion.'

Dhoble couldn't even disagree with this. As a policeman he, too, had survived on the same currency of money and information. The first had enabled him to buy the second and the second had led to a career full of successful arrests, seizures, glowing news reports and medals.

'How much longer, my young friend?' KD asked genially, as if they were waiting at a pav bhaji stall for their order.

'Almost done, almost done,' Nick said without looking up, his fingers flying over the keyboard.

Dhoble badly wanted a drink. As soon as this was over, he was going to take the rest of the bloody day off and get hammered.

'What about my money?' Dhoble asked. 'You promised me five mill—'

'I never forget my promises, my friend,' Khush Dil said. 'And you will get it within the first five minutes of us leaving this room. I could have done it right now in real time, but this room is so secure that no cell phones work here. Same reason why our young friend here has to copy the information on his computer and then relay it to the buyer, instead of directly sending it to the buyer's computer from here.'

Dhoble mulled over these words carefully for the next five minutes, saying nothing, his brain working furiously.

He was still thinking when Nick straightened up and said, 'Done!'

'Let's get out of here,' was all Dhoble said.

26

Ajay opened his eyes and immediately sprang out of bed, lunging for his phone.

For the last three days, ever since his violent confrontation with Asiya, he had only slept fitfully and always woken up fearing he had missed out on some important development in the investigation. During these three days, he had tapped every informant known to him, including some that he hadn't spoken to in years. He had also touched base with every friendly intelligence agency and even put out feelers to some not-so-friendly ones, with the exception of the ISI. To all of them, he had said the same thing – give me Asiya and name your price.

Of course, he knew that her name was a cover, as was her entire identity. But it was a damn good cover.

And, more importantly, her real identity seemed to be a complete mystery. No one seemed to know anything about this woman who was as dangerous as she was attractive.

The only information coming in was about the K-e-M. Ajay was astounded that the outfit's name had stayed secret for so long, despite having been active for over a year, if the intelligence he was getting was to be believed.

Ajay quickly scrolled through his messages and notifications while shaking off the last cobwebs of sleep from his head. Slipping the phone into the pocket of his shorts, he padded to the bathroom. He hadn't shaved in three days and there were dark circles around his eyes. He hadn't run a comb through his hair either.

He splashed cold water over his face several times, stared at his reflection and once again cursed himself for having fallen prey to Asiya's wiles. *The oldest trick in the book and I walked right into it.*

He walked out of the bathroom and stopped in his tracks, his right hand instinctively going to his back before realizing that his gun was in the drawer near his bed. He clenched his fists and planted his feet firmly into the ground.

The man in the living room of his officers' quarters was sitting calmly in a chair, one leg crossed over the other, a slight smile on his face. He was white –

obviously a Westerner – dressed in a loose shirt and baggy cargos. He was sitting casually, as if there was nothing wrong with him arriving uninvited into the official residence of a DIG-rank officer.

'Who are you?' Ajay snarled. 'How did you get in?'

'Come on, Ghazi,' Hoffman replied. 'I got you into Osama Bin Laden's house all those years ago. You think I can't get into yours?'

Ajay relaxed. Despite all his stress, he found himself smiling just a little.

'Goddammit, man,' he said, walking over and sitting in the other chair in the room. 'Nestor, wasn't it?'

'That was the codename I was using, yes.' Hoffman smiled. 'The powers that be didn't deem it fit for you to know my real identity at the time. Which is why we only spoke on the phone, using codenames.'

Ajay massaged his forehead.

'But you knew mine?'

'From the beginning. You were one of the men on the ground. Protocol required us to know everything about the men actually conducting the operation. I have big fat dossiers on you, as well as everyone else who set foot on Pakistani soil that night.'

'Seems like an aeon ago now, doesn't it?' Ajay said.

'Well, yes and no.'

Ajay looked at Hoffman suspiciously.

'Nestor ...'

'Hoffman,' the American replied. 'Jon Hoffman. You can call me Jon.'

'I'll call you Jeanie if that makes you happy, but that "yes and no" and your expression tells me you have some bad news. And you should know that I have my plate rather full with bad news right now,' Ajay said morosely.

'Then I must apologize in advance. But what I'm about to tell you is directly connected to the case you're investigating, as well as the operation we were part of twelve years ago.'

Ajay opened his mouth but no words came out. His current investigation into Asiya and … the operation to kill Osama Bin Laden? He tried to wrap his head around it but could not.

'It's a lot to take in, I know. Trust me, I couldn't believe it either.'

Hoffman waited till Ajay could speak again.

'You know who she is?' he finally asked.

Hoffman reached into one of the many pockets of his cargos and brought out a cell phone with a large screen, almost a small electronic tablet. He quickly powered up the screen and tapped out a series of commands as he started speaking.

'You know we have some pretty advanced facial recognition technology, right?' he said.

Ajay nodded. India was centuries behind when it came to the technology that the CIA had at its disposal.

'So, after this Asiya Khan attacked you and you guys sent out a discreet request to all agencies seeking information about her, we looked through our files but found nothing. Which was curious because somewhere, at some point, there had to be a trace, a sighting, a shadow, something. Very little misses our eyes, and I'm not even boasting here.'

Ajay only nodded and waited for the CIA agent to come to the point.

'So, we ran her face through our facial recognition software, which not only searches for a face as it looks today, but also in the past.'

Ajay leaned forward.

'Your facial recognition can remove age from a face?'

Hoffman nodded.

'Just like it can add age to a twelve-year-old photograph to see what the person might look like today, it can remove age to give you an idea of what they might have looked like years ago as well.'

'We've been trying to get that AI for years,' Ajay said. 'But the ones we sampled are simply not good enough. Apparently there's one in the market, but the inventor is damn elusive.'

Hoffman chuckled.

'The inventor is us,' he said. 'That's why we're elusive.'

'Fuckers,' Ajay responded, but he was smiling. He understood the need of every intelligence agency for exclusivity.

'So,' Hoffman resumed, 'we came up with several options. You know, five years, seven years, ten years. We stopped at fifteen years because Asiya would be in her early thirties now, if not late twenties, so that seemed a safe bet. Then we ran those photos through our records, and we got a hit for twelve years ago.'

Hoffman passed the tablet to Ajay. The Indian cop took it and looked keenly at the face on the screen. She was younger, but the eyes were the same, as was the shape of the lips. There was also a tiny mole on the right cheek. It was Asiya for sure.

'You know her real name?'

'Nobody knows her real name,' Hoffman replied. 'What we do know is that she was Osama Bin Laden's adopted daughter.

'Now, according to our records, Osama had ten daughters, two of whom were named Aasiah and Aisha. One of them – we do not which – was your lady love.'

A stunned Ajay looked up at Hoffman.

'Especially when you said that the woman also spoke fluent Urdu …' Hoffman continued talking while Ajay's mind trailed off, thinking about Asiya and her unique personality traits.

For a few minutes, neither man spoke. As the shock started ebbing, Ajay became aware of his cell phone buzzing in his pocket. He didn't seem to have the energy to reach for it but knew he had to. It could be important, maybe about Asiya.

With supreme effort, he took out the phone from his pocket and looked at the caller ID flashing on the screen.

It read 'Retd ACP M. Dhoble'.

27

It had been twelve years since her life changed forever. She remembered the night clearly – the early hours of 2 May 2011. The two MH-60 Black Hawk helicopters whirring above their mansion had signalled the beginning of the end for her foster father, the man she called Abba-jaan. The sound of the rotors in her head was so loud that she now wanted to cover her ears with her palms and become immune to the past, to pretend like none of it had happened. But that would mean betraying her Abba-jaan, it would mean betraying Osama Bin Laden.

She had never seen fear on her foster father's face until that night. Even when he'd sent the civilian aeroplanes crashing into the symbols of America's pride, his face had shown no emotion barring an all-knowing smile.

She was the daughter of one of Bin Laden's bodyguards. Her biological father had died while saving Bin Laden during the last phase of Russia's conflict with Afghanistan. To repay the debt, his master had taken her amongst his own children and never treated her differently from his own flesh and blood. Bin Laden had filled the void left by her father.

Abba-jaan was a man of great fecundity. He had sired twenty-three (known) children from five (known) wives. Fate had denied her direct descendancy from his lineage, but he had loved her far more than his ten daughters and thirteen sons. He had raised her as his favourite child, his protégée.

A sob choked her throat. Outside, the wind rustled through the poplar trees.

'My dear child,' he said. 'The hour has come.'

'The infidels shall pay for this grave misdeed,' she said. 'I will fight to my last breath.'

Bin Laden walked towards a wall and turned over the carpet to reveal a trapdoor. Asiya fervently hoped that her foster father would seek refuge in the deepest pits of the world, only to emerge safe and sound in another land. The fight would continue, after all.

But her worst fears came true when he pushed her down into the safety of the ventilator instead. For the first time ever, she looked upon her father with questioning eyes. He wanted to save her life and not his own!

'I am tired now. I cannot keep running.' He clasped her hand tightly. 'For the sake of the heavens, stay here until you are safe.'

She shook her head, crying. Tears rolled down her pink cheeks. He had given her an oath she could not break. She did not want to let go of him. But the trapdoor was slammed shut. She muffled her mouth with her hands and cried. The infidels were at the doorstep. A gap through a ventilator allowed her a partial view of the floor above.

The next few minutes passed in a blur. There was the sound of a door being broken down, and then gunfire, a lot of gunfire. More than was needed to kill a single man. This wasn't just a mission; it was an execution. She drew her knees close to her chest and hugged them, crying silently. She fought hard to keep her sobs quiet, although it felt as if her heart was going to burst out of her chest any second.

Already, through the haze of her grief, a new emotion was taking birth: hatred.

She watched as the black-clad soldiers bent down to examine the face of her fallen Abba-jaan, and told each other who he was. She could understand what they were saying; Bin Laden had spent months teaching her to read, write and speak English.

They straightened and bumped fists, celebrating the death of her father.

Then, another man entered. He, too, was clad in black and wearing a mask. He held a pistol in his right hand and was gripping his right wrist with his left hand.

The man started collecting DNA samples, and seemed familiar. His eyes were brown and intense, and when he took off his gloves for a brief moment, she noticed a scar on his thumb. She tried to recollect. Where had she seen this man before?

In this house, of course! He had accompanied someone. Yes, this man had carried the bag for the doctor who had vaccinated Abu Ahmed's son. Her heart burned with the heat of a thousand volcanoes. An American may have fired the bullet but this man, who was now grinning behind the mask, had enabled her Abba-jaan's death. He must have provided the Americans with the information which had led to the death of the Shaikh.

She had cursed him with every ounce of emotion back then, because there was nothing else she could do. But times would change, she was sure of that.

The men zipped up her fallen father inside a black body bag and carried it away. Soon, she again heard sound of a chopper's blades. People had gathered outside the mansion and were shouting.

Drenched in sweat, still crying inside the Abbottabad compound, Asiya swore upon the heavens one more time. Every breath she took after this dark night would be a debt that could be repaid only by annihilating the man and the nation which had enabled the killing of her father.

She was left an orphan in a big bad world, where she would be treated like a pariah. But she would not wallow in self-pity; she would not lead a life of orphanhood. She would let the world know that she was the daughter of the world's deadliest anarchist. Soon, she would be recognized as the Black Orphan.

'Aa gaya, Madam.'

The taxi driver's voice jolted Asiya out of her reverie. She quickly paid him and got out of the taxi.

It was late morning, but the Worli Sea Face was teeming with people. Some were running, some strolling, others simply sitting and enjoying the cool wind in their faces. A few couples were sitting cosily nestled against each other, oblivious to the world around them.

Asiya found an empty bench and sat down. She opened the laptop she was carrying and started her cell phone's hotspot.

Just as the computer connected to the internet, she received a text from Nick.

'I'm here. You ready?'

'Yes,' she replied and waited.

Today would be the first step of her revenge. All the nuclear plans developed by India after years of research would be in her hands and would go directly to the ISI. Pakistan's scientists would waste no time in creating a nuclear weapon of their own, based on the research. Already, several terrorist outfits were ready to pump money by the billions into the manufacturing process. And the only three scientists who could have created any kind of countermeasure for the weapons were dead, killed by her.

And then she would turn her entire attention to Ajay Rajvardhan.

28

Nick ran his eye over the lobby of the three-star hotel in Worli as he finished hacking the hotel's Wi-Fi connection. For someone of his capabilities, it was child's play. He had purposely chosen the hotel as scores of people would be using its Wi-Fi at any given point in time, just as Asiya had chosen the Worli Sea Face because she knew it would be crowded. They were reasonably close to each other.

Nick opened the folder containing the files he had copied from the IARC server less than an hour ago. Using a secure file-sharing software, he started sending the data to Asiya, who was also using the same software. It would run all the data through heavy encryption before sending the files, and anyone wishing to access it would need a decryption key, which only Asiya had.

The software worked fast but the data was heavy. It would still take some time.

The process had just started when two men slid onto the sofa he was sitting on, one on either side. At that very instant, he felt something cold and hard being jammed against the right side of his stomach, while a hand was placed around his shoulder.

He whirled his head to his left to see Dhoble sitting next to him, his expression grim. He turned to his right and saw Ajay, his left arm around Nick's shoulder and right hand holding the pistol poking him. He recognized the cop from the news.

'Stop whatever you're doing,' Ajay said in a low voice.

Nick's fingers froze over the keyboard.

'Look around you,' Ajay went on. Nick obeyed. All around the lobby, security personnel clad in dark suits were approaching the people and politely but firmly herding them out.

'Soon, it's going to be just the three of us in this lobby. Which means you don't get to pull any tricks. No taking advantage of the crowds to try and escape, no pulling any alarms and starting a stampede. Plus, if you so much as twitch without my permission, I will put a bullet in your stomach. And you have no idea how much that hurts.'

Nick had never been shot before and he sure as hell didn't wish to find out how it felt.

'Wh … what do you want?'

'What exactly is it that you're doing?' Ajay asked.

Nick told him.

'Okay, keep doing that. Where is she?'

'Worli Sea Face.'

'Where exactly?'

'I … I don't know … honest … I don't know …'

Ajay pressed the gun a little harder.

'I really don't know!' Nick hissed, wincing in pain.

'How long will this process take? Roughly?'

'Around an hour, maybe,' Nick replied, still gritting his teeth due to the pain.

'Can you slow it down?'

'Not … not without making her suspicious. And she will kill me if I make her suspicious. You don't know her …'

'Oh, I do,' Ajay said, wryly, glancing around at the almost empty lobby just as his phone buzzed. He took the call.

'We got Khush Dil,' Pratap said from the other end. 'And we have his cell phone with Dhoble's little performance on it. They're bringing him to Crime Branch headquarters right now.'

'Great, sir.'

'I'm sending every available unit to you.'

'Very quietly, sir. This woman is extremely dangerous.'

'Got it,' Pratap said and ended the call.

Ajay stood up.

'You have that gun I gave you?' he asked Dhoble.

The retired cop drew the gun out.

'If this little bastard tries anything, shoot him,' Ajay said.

'With pleasure, sir,' Dhoble growled.

Ajay bent down and brought his face level with Nick's.

'Listen to me carefully,' he said. 'What you have on your computer is top-secret classified data. And Dhoble is going to testify to his role. Which means we have you on an Official Secrets charge AND a terrorism charge. Your only hope in hell is to cooperate. Understand?'

Nick could only nod.

Ajay ran out of the hotel and into the car, where Hoffman was waiting in the driver's seat with the engine running.

Ajay had first met Dhoble at an interagency conference when the latter was with the Mumbai Anti-Narcotics Cell.

One of the subjects under discussion had been narco-terrorism. Ajay had delivered a talk about how money earned through the illegal heroin trade was funnelled all the way to Afghanistan, to the Taliban's pockets, and had urged officers with anti-narcotics cells to look beyond just street peddlers. He had exchanged numbers with Dhoble at the end of the conference, and they had kept in touch off and on.

When Dhoble had called Ajay while he was talking to Hoffman, Ajay had initially ignored the call. It was only when the retired cop had called thrice without respite that Ajay had answered. But what Dhoble told him spurred him into action. Dhoble didn't know about the murders of the three IARC scientists, but Ajay and Hoffman did, and they immediately made the connection. It was, after all, too much of a coincidence that someone was stealing data from the IARC just after their three top scientists had been murdered. And the murderer, beyond doubt, was Asiya, which meant that whoever had stolen the data was connected to her.

Dhoble had called from his car while following Khush Dil and Nick at a safe distance and also relayed their car's licence plate number to Ajay.

Hoffman and Ajay immediately set out, armed and ready. After Khush Dil dropped Nick at the hotel, Ajay passed on the licence plate number to Pratap and entered the hotel with Dhoble.

As they were entering the hotel, Dhoble said, 'I have done a lot of bad things in my life, Ajay sir. But even I have limits.'

'That's not going to get you out of this mess, Dhoble,' Ajay replied.

'I know, sir,' Dhoble admitted, 'and I'll face whatever is coming to me.'

Now, Ajay slid into the passenger seat beside Hoffman. The American asked, 'Where to?'

'Straight ahead till you see the promenade,' Ajay replied.

Hoffman swore. He immediately computed the fact that the promenade would have tons of civilians and tracking and apprehending Asiya in their midst was going to be a nightmare.

'Go to the end and take a U-turn so that we're on the same side as the Sea Face,' Ajay said. 'After that, we'll have to cruise slowly and hope we spot her.'

'You have a plan?' Hoffman asked.

'The plan is to stop her, Jon,' Ajay replied grimly.

Hoffman steadily depressed the accelerator.

29

Asiya checked on the status of the file transfer and noted with satisfaction that it was almost 50 per cent done. She let her thoughts go back to Ajay.

She could clearly see the corridors of the Abbottabad haveli in her head. She remembered the compounder who would often accompany the general physician when called to vaccinate the children of the house. She was still a teenager, and he was a rather good-looking young man.

She would watch him from behind her veil, or when she was half hidden behind the curtains or the walls. The woman of the household did not remove their purdah in front of strangers. She would giggle at the sight of him. He had a huge scar on the thumb of his right hand, like a bullet wound. His brown eyes were *intense*, and though he would constrain his movements, she could sense that he was looking out for something … someone. She wondered if he was looking out for her.

She was horrified when she saw the same intense eyes and scarred thumb amongst the men who had breached their mansion with C-60 explosives. He had carried a gun. And though he hadn't fired the killing shots, he was still the man who had led the American forces to their hideout. He had thrust a dagger in Bin Laden's back.

'I think I see her,' Hoffman said.

'You sure?' Ajay asked.

'No, but there's a woman ahead about the same build, with a laptop.'

'Keep driving. Stop a couple of hundred metres ahead. We'll come back on foot.'

Hoffman stopped by the side of the road, pulling up the handbrake and opening his door in one motion. Ajay also got out and together they were about to start walking when a shrill whistle pierced the air, followed by a yell.

Both men turned to see a traffic policeman coming up to them indignantly.

'You see that?' the cop asked in Hindi, pointing to a 'No Parking' sign just a couple of feet from where Hoffman had parked. 'It's in English. Easy to read. Big letters. What's the problem?'

The cop turned to Hoffman.

'You can read English, right?' he said, switching from Hindi to English.

Hoffman caught the sarcasm in his voice.

'There is no need to be facetious, sir,' he snapped.

At that very instant, Ajay pulled out his NIA ID card and stuck it under the cop's nose.

'If you do not stop yelling right fucking now,' Ajay swore, 'I will have you dismissed from service.'

After Bin Laden's death, Asiya was smuggled into India and raised by Hafsa, who was one of Bin Laden's associates, running a sleeper network in the country without even causing a blip on the authorities' radar. Hafsa recognized the fire burning within Asiya and inducted her into the K-e-M. Asiya aced the training phase, putting every other recruit to shame, and came back as a walking weapon of destruction. She had also spent her training days intently following the news from India. A small, largely speculative news report about India working on a nuclear programme caught her attention and by the time she returned, she had a plan ready. She told Hafsa her plan and at that moment, the old woman knew that she had found the perfect protégée.

The terrified traffic cop got into Hoffman's vehicle and drove it away as the agents started walking towards the spot where they thought they had seen Asiya. As they advanced, slowly and carefully, they could see uniformed policemen forming a loose, inconspicuous cordon around the promenade. Pratap seemed to have issued his instructions. To a trained cop's eye, the police presence was visibly increasing. Ajay was sure there were more cops in plainclothes around as well.

'I see her,' he said in a low voice.

'It's her, right?' Hoffman asked.

They walked a few more steps and Ajay could now see her clearly. He hated himself for the slight tug at his heart.

'It is her,' he said and stepped up his pace.

Hoffman fell into step behind him.

Ajay pulled out his cell phone and called Pratap.

'I'm on my way, Ajay,' the senior cop said. 'I should be there in ten minutes.'

'Okay, but I need the cops here to hang back till Asiya is neutralized. This can turn into a bloodbath.'

'Agreed. I'll tell them.'

Ajay ended the call and walked up to where Asiya was sitting. She must have felt him approach because she suddenly looked up sharply as he came to a stop in front of her.

'So, you found me,' she said, hatred blazing in her eyes.

'It's over, Asiya,' Ajay replied. 'We have the hacker and Khush Dil. Teams are on their way to pick up your ISI contact as we speak. We know everything.'

Asiya smiled a slow, deliberate smile.

'Everything? You sure?'

'Yes,' Ajay replied. 'We know about your father too.'

Asiya's smile turned into a snarl. She leaned forward and instantly, Ajay whipped out his gun and pointed it straight at her. Hoffman, too, moved forward, his own gun appearing in his hand, pointed straight at Asiya.

As expected, the sight of the guns immediately sparked off panic among the people nearby. The policemen who had been hanging back immediately moved in. They all knew who Ajay was and had been briefed about the mission, and that he had a foreign government agent with him.

Quickly and efficiently, the cops started shepherding the public away from the spot. Some of them drew their guns on Asiya as well, but, due to the sheer number of civilians around, most of them had to focus on crowd control.

'You came well prepared,' Asiya said.

'Yes, I did. Now raise your hands.'

Asiya slowly raised both her hands above her head, extending her arms all the way. Then she did something unexpected. She curled her hands into fists, letting only the thumbs stick out, holding out a two thumbs-up sign high over her head.

Before Ajay could react, a shot rang out and Hoffman dropped to the ground, blood streaming from a bullet wound to his head.

30

In the split second during which Ajay jerked his head to look at the fallen Hoffman, Asiya made her move. She slammed the laptop shut and used it to bat the gun out of Ajay's hands. The impact of the blow made him stumble.

He immediately whirled back to her but she used the laptop as a weapon again, aiming for his head. Ajay threw both arms up and blocked the blow, but it knocked him off-balance.

At the same time, ten members of the K-e-M came out of the crowd and started firing at the cops. The civilians started running helter-skelter. Complete chaos descended on the Sea Face.

A police car came up, siren blaring, and screeched to a hard stop. Pratap jumped out, gun drawn, and ran towards the battle. As a uniformed constable fell with two bullet wounds to his torso, Pratap let out a yell and fired at the woman he had spotted emptying her gun at the constable. The woman went down in a hail of rounds.

Even amid the pandemonium, Ajay and Pratap let their training and experience kick in. They stole quick glances at the women shooting at them and took in their attire. All of them were dressed in loose T-shirts with a prominent logo and cargos. Within one second, both cops had computed the information: look out for black T-shirts with logos.

For a moment it seemed like 26/11 once again, this time with young women unleashing their vendetta against Indian civilians.

Asiya ran to the edge of the promenade and tossed the laptop towards the sea. It landed hard on the tetrapods and shattered to pieces. She turned back just as Ajay came running and tackled him head-on. They both went down in a tangle, Ajay's hands clawing at her face. Asiya gripped his hands, wrested them away and head-butted Ajay on the nose repeatedly till she felt the cartilage shatter.

She stood up and ran towards the Bandra–Worli Sea Link. She knew Ajay wouldn't be far behind, but she had the tiniest head start and that was enough.

Three of her sisters from the K-e-M saw her and broke off to defend her. They stepped directly into Ajay's path and trained their guns on him.

Running behind Ajay, Pratap took aim and shot. One of the three women went down. The other two immediately shifted their attention to him. Pratap and Ajay both hit the ground and started rolling sideways. Pratap managed to get another shot and took out another terrorist.

The third one advanced, firing, and was almost on top of Pratap when she was shot in the head. Pratap and Ajay both straightened to see Dhoble advancing, holding Ajay's back-up gun. He tossed the gun to Ajay and picked up the fallen terrorist's handgun.

'Go!' Pratap said to Ajay as he and Dhoble came together, their backs pressed to each other, guns raised.

Ajay checked the ammunition clip, wiped the blood streaming from his nose and started running.

Another K-e-M terrorist came running straight for Ajay and without stopping, he raised his gun and put a bullet squarely in her forehead. She was dead before she hit the ground.

In the distance, he saw Asiya run on to the Sea Link. He quickened his pace and got to the entrance to the Sea Link just as Asiya let loose a volley of shots, sending cars skidding out of control. Within minutes, the Sea Link was filled with cars that had stopped where they were, some straight, some sideways. The entire bridge became an obstacle course of vehicles even as people started pouring out of the cars and running for their lives.

Ajay fought against the tide of humanity, his gun half raised, finger on the trigger, struggling to get a glimpse of Asiya. He weaved in and out of the crowd, eyes alert, and was almost at the middle of the Sea Link when a shot rang out and he felt something whizz past his side.

He immediately jumped behind an abandoned car and bent low as two more shots slammed into the car's chassis.

He risked a quick peek over the car's hood and saw Asiya standing dead in the centre of the Sea Link, gun aimed straight at him.

'Come out, you bastard!' she screamed. 'Come out and face your death!'

She walked forward, shooting at the car that Ajay was crouched behind. She kept shooting till her gun was empty.

'Come on!' she yelled furiously, slapping a fresh clip into her pistol.

Ajay sprang up and let loose a volley of shots. Asiya simply dropped to the ground, rolled and came back up on her knees in one fluid movement, her gun aimed at him. Ajay ducked again, cursing.

'Talk to me, Ajay Rajvardhan!' Asiya called out. 'Tell me how much you love me, how I am the most beautiful woman you've ever seen. Quote some philosophy to me. Come on, charmer!'

Ajay gritted his teeth and stood up again, firing his gun as he moved. He emptied his entire clip at Asiya, who ducked and dodged and all the time kept walking up to him.

Finally, there was a click as Ajay's gun ran out of rounds. He stood rooted to the ground, while Asiya stopped as well, her gun aimed at his head. He dropped his pistol and stared into her eyes.

'Do it,' he said. 'Go on, fire.'

Asiya lowered her gun. Pointing it straight at the ground near her feet, she squeezed the trigger again and again, not flinching as lead crashed into concrete and sparks flew furiously. Then she let the empty gun fall to the ground.

She clenched her fists and started walking. Ajay looked back. Pratap, Dhoble and the other cops were still busy trading fire with the other K-e-M members. It was just the two of them now.

Ajay planted his feet firmly on the ground and brought his hands up in a fighting stance. Asiya only smiled as she leapt off the ground, her right leg knifing forward in a kick.

Ajay blocked her attack, but the force threw him backwards. He caught himself and jumped at her, going for her throat. She caught both his hands, pulled him towards her and ramming her knee into his abdomen.

He fell to the ground, and she was on him like a wildcat, punching, clawing, kicking. He fought back but was no match for her training, skill and, most of all, her anger.

He managed to grab one of her hands but she immediately clutched his throat with the other. She brought her face close to his.

'You think this is bad?' she snarled. 'Wait till I'm done with you. After that, I'm going for your beloved country. I'm going to inflict on your homeland a fate far worse than the one you gave my Abbu-jaan.'

Ajay looked into her eyes and in an instant, knew that she meant it. There was only one thing to be done.

With all his might, he managed to slip one leg between them and kicked hard, throwing her off. She hit her head on the ground as she fell, but rolled over and stood up. The blow to the head, however, had slowed her down by just a few seconds.

Ajay used those precious seconds to stand up and move faster than he had ever done in his life. As Asiya also stood up, he ran around her and got behind her. Before she could turn, he enveloped her in a bear hug, clasping his arms around her torso, trapping her in his embrace.

Asiya screamed and kicked like a bucking horse, but Ajay held fast and dragged her to the edge of the Sea Link. She was still screaming when he took a deep breath, braced his leg against an abandoned car and heaved backwards.

They fell straight into the sea below.

31

Pratap was locked in deadly hand-to-hand combat with the last of the K-e-M terrorists.

He had run out of ammo and taken a shot in his forearm from the terrorist's gun before throwing himself on her, making her gun fall.

The terrorist grabbed his shirt lapel and tried to bite him, while he held her at bay with both hands. She shifted her hands to his throat just as Dhoble came up from behind, grabbed her and threw her against the promenade railing.

She hit her head and fell to the ground, lifeless.

Pratap stood up and looked at the Sea Link just in time to see Ajay and Asiya drop off the bridge.

He checked his gunshot wound. The bullet had only grazed his forearm. He was losing blood but would be fine for a few minutes. Dhoble saw it too and within seconds, tied his handkerchief around Pratap's forearm as tight as he could.

Pratap vaulted over the railing and onto the tetrapods below. He started jumping from one tetrapod to another, making his way towards the water as fast as he could.

Meanwhile, as he fell, Ajay's mind quickly computed his situation. His nose was shattered and he was no longer able to breathe through it. He had been breathing through his mouth the last few minutes.

The sea came rushing up to meet him and he let go of Asiya, drawing the longest of breaths through his mouth just as he felt his body slam against the bed of water.

He sank deep, opened his eyes and forced himself to focus on the last bit of information he had taken in just before entering the water: Asiya had a small knife tucked in her boot. He had seen it when the leg of her jeans hiked up as she fell.

He swam towards her dim form. Already, he could see her regain her bearings and look around for him. He didn't stand a chance against her in fair hand-to-hand combat, much less underwater.

He dived low and went for her leg. The only thing that worked in his favour was that she didn't realize what he was doing. Before she could understand, he slipped the knife out of her boot. Then he kicked several times and swam upwards and away from her.

Both came up to the surface almost at the same time. For a moment, they bobbed up and down, treading water, before starting to swim towards each other.

'Hang on, Ajay!' he heard Pratap call out from a distance. 'I'm coming!'

Ajay didn't have time to hang on. Asiya lunged and planted both her hands firmly on his shoulders. With all her might, she pushed him down just as he drew another long breath.

Ajay went down without a fight, but as he dipped he buried the knife in her abdomen. Even from under the water, he could hear her scream. Asiya let go of his shoulders and as he came up, she swung her fist, catching him in the side of his head.

Ajay took the blow. His priority was only to keep holding on to the knife. Gritting his teeth, he pulled the knife out and rammed it in again, making a fresh wound in her stomach.

Asiya kept staring at him, eyes full of vicious hatred, even as he twisted the knife in her belly. She raised both hands and gripped his throat. She was no longer trying to drown him. Instead, she was using all the strength she had left to strangle him.

And it was working. Ajay could feel his oxygen supply being cut off. He was choking and getting dizzy.

He struggled hard to focus. His free hand clutched Asiya's shoulder. Her eyes kept boring into his as she kept squeezing, not letting up at all.

With one supreme effort, he tightened his loosening grip around the knife's smooth, cold handle, removed it from her stomach and drove it up.

The last thing he saw before he passed out was the blade getting buried in the soft flesh just under her chin. His fingers opened and released his grip around the knife's handle.

The world started closing in around Ajay as his eyes rolled up in their sockets and he started sinking to the bottom.

His last thought was, *is she dead?*

Then everything went black.

32

Juanita Martinez walked quickly and with purpose, her boots making a dull thud on the tiled floor as she advanced towards the conference room at the NIA office in Mumbai.

Her official title was senior analyst with the Central Intelligence Agency. It was, however, just a title. Over the last fifteen years, the fifty-something veteran spy had been responsible for some of the deadliest and dirtiest missions in countries across the globe. Her most recent assignment had been in India, where she was directly handling the day-to-day activities of one Jonathan Hoffman, recently killed in action on Indian soil.

Unlike most of her peers, Martinez didn't dress in crisp suits and heels. She preferred cargos, T-shirts and jackets, with heavy leather boots. It was what she would wear as a young operative on the field and what she felt comfortable in. Just because she had traded battlefields in war zones for ones in office buildings, it was no reason to hang up her battle fatigues.

Martinez pushed open the door to the conference room. DIG Ajay, Joint Commissioner of Police Pratap, Mumbai Police Commissioner Kumar and National Security Advisor Nishikant Dobriyal were sitting around a large table. Martinez took the chair closest to Ajay and leaned back, her fingers lightly drumming the table.

'Good to see you back in action, Mr Rajvardhan,' she said.

'Ajay, please. It's good to be back. All thanks to Pratap sir.'

Pratap only smiled. He had managed to swim up to Ajay just as he was about to go under and dragged him to the shore. It took another couple of hours for divers to reach the scene and pull Asiya's body out. Ajay, despite his injuries, had not moved from the edge of the water till he saw the body and heard the doctor officially pronounce her dead. Only then did he allow the paramedics to lead him away. He still had a bandage on his nose and a whole range of bruises from Asiya's merciless blows.

'And this Asiya Khan, she is confirmed dead?' Martinez asked.

'I've seen the body. She is dead beyond doubt,' Ajay replied.

'I want to see the body.'

'Sure, sure,' NSA Dobriyal said, standing up. 'May I offer you coffee?'

'I'd rather come straight to the point, please,' Martinez replied. 'One of our men was killed in your country. That kind of thing has repercussions.'

Before Dobriyal could respond, Ajay spoke up.

'If I may, Ms Martinez, Hoffman died in action on a mission of supreme importance not just to India but also to USA and any other country that is currently fighting the bane of terrorism. He went beyond the call of duty and laid down his life trying to apprehend a dreaded terrorist.'

'I'm aware of all of that. And I can also read the subtext in your words, Ajay. You're subtly telling me that he became part of your operation when he had no need to do so and that, in a way, his death was his own fault.'

'I didn't say that,' Ajay said.

'And I'm not stupid,' Martinez shot back. 'We'd like access to Asiya's ISI contact that you've arrested.'

The trace programme that Ajay had put on his substitute laptop, which Asiya had accessed in the seven-star hotel that night, had led the NIA to an ISI sleeper agent based in south Mumbai, who had been feeding intelligence to Pakistan for a decade. He was currently in NIA custody, picked up shortly after Asiya's death. And he was singing like a canary.

'By all means,' Dobriyal said. 'We'd be happy to share whatever we get from him.'

'Not good enough,' Martinez said. 'I need to interrogate him personally.'

For a minute, there was silence in the room. Then, Ajay spoke up again.

'Suppose,' he said, 'you start with a little gesture of good faith?'

'I'm not sure any more good faith is required on my part, but what is it that you were hoping to get from me?' Martinez said curtly.

'How about Operation Dark Ages?' Ajay said.

For the first time, Martinez looked thrown. Her face, which had till then been set in a slight scowl, went stony.

Ajay picked up a water bottle and finished it in one gulp.

'You've heard of Moshe Frischman, I presume? The Israeli national who was found murdered in Colaba?' he asked as he set the empty bottle down.

Martinez nodded.

'He was a Mossad agent, but then I'm sure you knew that already. He was also my friend. And the last person he met on the day that he died was Jonathan Hoffman.'

Martinez said nothing. It was impossible to gauge how much she already knew.

'Moshe left a message for me on his computer, which I discovered the morning after his murder. It simply said, "Operation Dark Ages". I searched high and low, tapping my sources in Pakistan and the Middle East, to find out what it meant, and no one seemed to have heard anything. Finally, I retraced his steps on the day of his murder. The usual methods – CCTV and cellular location tracking. Which is how I found out about his meeting with Hoffman.'

Martinez was still silent.

'So I looked in the one place I hadn't so far. I had simply assumed that it was connected to India and Israel's common enemies, but I never thought it might be connected to India's *friends.* And we both know we have more sources in each other's agencies than we care to let on. That's how I found out that Dark Ages was a CIA operation.'

Martinez spoke for the first time.

'I have no idea what …'

'You will kindly do me the favour of not sitting in my own house and lying to my face, Ms Martinez,' NSA Dobriyal spoke up for the first time.

'We have found out,' Dobriyal continued, 'and confirmed through various sources, including Asiya's ISI contact, that a large amount of money had been committed to the ISI for the development of nuclear weapons, which were to be created with the help of the data stolen from our research facility. This money was coming from outside Pakistan through a whole network of shell companies and dummy corporations. But it all comes down to five organizations based in the Middle East. And all five are controlled by the CIA.'

Martinez's olive skin turned a shade darker. Her hands were curled into loose fists. She wasn't a woman who liked to be caught napping.

'Classic false flag approach,' Ajay said. 'You approached the ISI through those five front companies and offered to finance their nuclear programme if they could steal our research. Even the ISI didn't know that they were dealing with the CIA.'

'It was never supposed to ...' Martinez started speaking but stopped. Then she spoke again. 'They were ... the ISI was never supposed to actually make any weapons. We had plans in place to ensure that.'

'Of course you did,' Dobriyal snapped. 'The plan was to deal a blow to India's nuclear progress as well as keep Pakistan out of the race at the same time. To keep both countries in the dark ages.'

'And for good reason,' Martinez snapped back. 'Every time one of you makes a nuclear weapon, the other countries are thrown into a panic. The race intensifies. The demand for radioactive materials goes up. The demand for black market nukes goes up. The whole fucking ecosystem is thrown off-balance.'

'So, only the great US of A is allowed to be a nuclear god, is it? The rest of us have to meekly stay in line and respect the status quo?' Dobriyal asked acerbically.

'It's not like that and you know it,' Martinez said, scowling.

'What we know,' Ajay said, cutting in, 'is that your own agent, Hoffman, was not comfortable with your plans. Which was why he talked about them to Moshe, knowing fully well he would come to me.'

'And you know that how?' Martinez asked.

'Because Hoffman told me as much. The day he came to my house. The day he was killed. And Moshe, minutes before he was shot dead, entered that message into his computer for me to find. That's two good agents lost, Ms Martinez. And their blood is on your hands.'

'So excuse me for not granting you any access to the ISI contact we have arrested,' Dobriyal added. 'But I really don't feel very cooperative right now.'

'Gentleman, you're missing the point. The operation was never meant to take any lives ...'

'But it did. And I don't know why you're missing that point. People have died. You got into bed with the K-e-M to achieve your objective and the K-e-M shed the blood of so many innocents in my country. Just like you people got into bed with the Taliban all those years ago, something that the world is still paying the price for,' Dobriyal said angrily.

Martinez looked away.

'I'd like to take Hoffman back to his family.'

'Hoffman's body is embalmed and in a coffin, waiting at a military installation in Mumbai. It will be driven to the international airport with a military escort and put on a plane without any red tape. Instructions have already been issued to that effect. The people in charge of the coffin see him as a fellow soldier and will treat him that way till he is in their hands,' Dobriyal replied.

Martinez stood up and walked out of the room.

EPILOGUE

The air was chilly, but the kahwa provided some warmth.

The woman on the tiny hillock stretched her legs and leaned back.

Around 200 metres away, twenty-five young women were crawling on the ground on their elbows and knees. At one end of the row, six bearded and turbanned men were kneeling with their AK-47 assault rifles, raised at eye level. They kept squeezing off shots straight ahead at irregular intervals. Any woman who straightened up without permission was at full risk of being shot dead, and the women on the ground were fully aware of this.

The sound of gunfire wasn't new to anyone living in that region. They had lived with that sound for decades and would probably continue to do so. Peace was something that the people here had long since given up on.

The public execution of Asiya Khan, whose real name was still not known to anyone, had spurred a new batch of recruits to join the K-e-M. It had been a month since the bloodbath at the Worli Sea Face in Mumbai. Thanks to the internet, hundreds of women had found the K-e-M's discussion forum on the dark web and expressed interest in laying down their lives for the cause. After careful and repeated screening, twenty-five of them had been selected and welcomed into the fold with the most glowing of words. Money was sent to them, tickets were booked and they were made to feel important and special in every possible way. That is till they reached the training camp in Afghanistan.

There they were given coarse uniforms to wear and thrown together in a tent. Their training, which was unforgiving and relentless, began the same day.

Sitting at her vantage point atop the hillock, Hafsa watched with satisfaction as the first batch of Sipahane Ayesha (Soldiers of Ayesha) were trained.

ABOUT THE AUTHOR

Before becoming a writer, publisher, producer, scriptwriter and mentor to new talent, S. Hussain Zaidi was a journalist for over twenty years. He started his career with *The Asian Age* and *The Indian Express* before moving on to *Mid-Day* and *Mumbai Mirror* as editor (investigations). He bid adieu to journalism in 2016.

His first book, *Black Friday,* was made into a critically acclaimed film by director Anurag Kashyap. His documentation of the Mumbai mafia in books such as *Dongri to Dubai*, *Mafia Queens of Mumbai*, *My Name Is Abu Salem* and *Byculla to Bangkok* is considered to be among some of the finest pieces of investigative journalism. His mastery over terrorism-related research is reflected in *Black Friday*, *Headley and I* and *Mumbai Avengers. Mumbai Avengers* was the first fiction title that Zaidi experimented with. The book was adapted into the Hindi film *Phantom*, starring Saif Ali Khan and Katrina Kaif and directed by Kabir Khan.

Zaidi was also associate producer, along with Dan Reed, of the documentary *Terror in Mumbai*, based on the 26/11 Mumbai attacks, for HBO. The movie was widely acclaimed and won a number of awards. While *Class of '83*, based on his book by the same name and produced by Shah Rukh Khan, is already streaming on Netflix, a web series based on *Dongri to Dubai*, being produced by Farhan Akhtar, will soon be released on Amazon Prime Video.

ALSO BY S. HUSSAIN ZAIDI

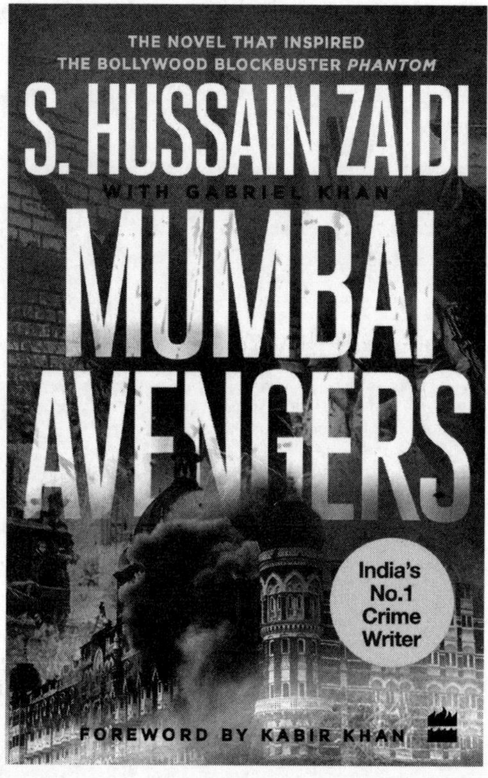

Five years after 26/11, India still seeks justice. The terrorists who planned it have disappeared into the darkness and Mumbai seethes with fury. One man will stop at nothing in his quest to avenge the dastardly act. Retired Lt Gen. Sayed Ali Waris of the Indian army masterminds a covert mission with a team of daredevil agents. As Waris and his team navigate untold dangers towards a nail-biting climax, will Mumbai finally be avenged?

ISBN: 9789351363682 Price: ₹350

'A gripping thriller with one twist after another.' – ***DNA***

It is nine years since the 26/11 terror attacks in Mumbai. In Bhopal, five members of the Indian Mujahideen break out of jail. Meanwhile, a retired schoolteacher, a heartbroken ex-soldier and a young woman board a cruise liner from Mumbai to Lakshadweep, which is hijacked. What is the connection between the escaped terrorists and the cruise liner? Will SP Vikrant Singh and his mentor Shahwaz Ali Mirza stop them in time? Racy and riveting, this is Hussain Zaidi at his best.

ISBN: 9789352779291 Price: ₹299

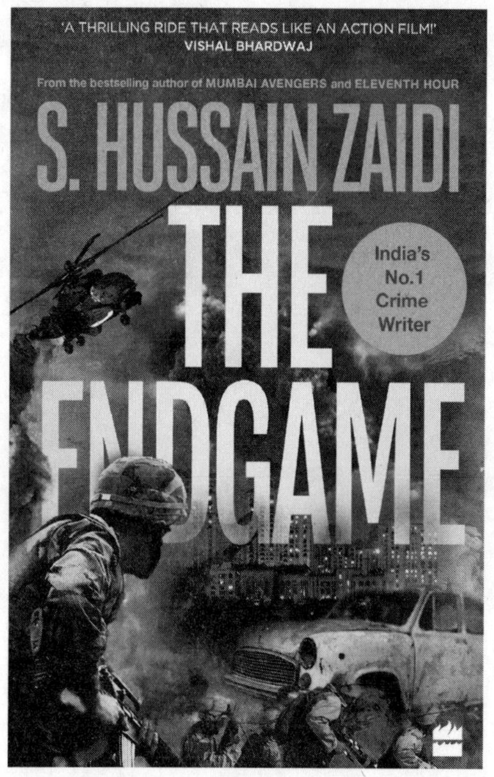

It's been three years since Shahwaz Ali Mirza and Vikrant Singh foiled dreaded terrorist Munafiq's attempt to leak State secrets from a naval server in Lakshadweep. But soon, the entire team from the Lakshadweep operation finds itself getting together for a new mission …

Hussain Zaidi is back with his irresistible cast of characters from *Eleventh Hour* in this sizzling story of politics, betrayal and unimaginable terror.

ISBN: 9789353578138 Price: ₹299

Mumbai is in a state of chaos. All the traffic signals across the city have stopped working.

A move by Vikrant Singh and Shahwaz Ali Mirza to bring forward the hacker who caused this backfires, leading to a second, bigger attack on Mumbai's lifeline, the railways.

It is their first brush with cyberterrorism – a zero-day vulnerability in the Indian government's system that could bring the country to its knees …

In *Zero Day*, Mirza and Vikrant face the most dangerous mission of their lives.

ISBN: 9789354893650 Price: ₹299

HarperCollins *Publishers* India

At HarperCollins India, we believe in telling the best stories and finding the widest readership for our books in every format possible. We started publishing in 1992; a great deal has changed since then, but what has remained constant is the passion with which our authors write their books, the love with which readers receive them, and the sheer joy and excitement that we as publishers feel in being a part of the publishing process.

Over the years, we've had the pleasure of publishing some of the finest writing from the subcontinent and around the world, including several award-winning titles and some of the biggest bestsellers in India's publishing history. But nothing has meant more to us than the fact that millions of people have read the books we published, and that somewhere, a book of ours might have made a difference.

As we look to the future, we go back to that one word—a word which has been a driving force for us all these years.

Read.